ROMANCING THE TREASURE

Survive the Romance #1

CAMI CHECKETTS

Birch River
PUBLISHING

COPYRIGHT

Romancing the Treasure: Survive the Romance #1

Copyright © 2021 by Cami Checketts

Edited by Daniel Coleman, Ceara Nobles, and Wendy Davy

FREE BOOK

Receive a free copy of *Seeking Mr. Debonair: The Jane Austen Pact* by clicking here and signing up for Cami's newsletter.

PROLOGUE

Britton Grady glanced around at his men—rather, former men. The eight of them had retired from active duty separately over the past few months. The other eight in their platoon were still in the service. Britton missed it. He knew his seven close friends felt the same. They were all trying to move on with their lives, start charities or businesses, date, and re-enter their families' lives, but it was tougher than he thought it'd be.

Tonight, their new normal might get flipped on its head by an intriguing offer. A reality TV show that matched an ex-military man with a charitably minded woman and put them in extreme situations for a week. Interesting, but was it interesting enough for all of them to commit?

"Fifty thousand dollars for a week?" Denzel asked in a bored, unemotional voice. Denzel had been nicknamed "Professor" because he was so cultured and refined—from the way he spoke and his extensive vocabulary to his smooth brown skin, piercing dark eyes, and ultra-handsome face. He looked like he could give

Idris Elba a run for his money as the next James Bond, especially because Denzel had an affinity for business suits and the Walther P99.

The beautiful blonde—Emerald Taylor, she'd introduced herself as—stood before them and smiled smoothly. "Yes, gentlemen. Fifty thousand dollars for only one week of your time."

"What's the catch?" Eli asked.

"No catch." Emerald gestured around the room. Ace hadn't closed his mouth fully since she'd walked in. Brit was waiting for one of the guys to notice and harass him. "My employer wants tough, experienced, good-looking men for this reality show. You'll each protect one woman in a location of my employer's choosing. Some of you will have to get from point A to point B, some will just have to make the best of whatever situation you're dropped into. Each situation will be vastly different, some more dangerous or miserable than others, but you will each be paid fifty thousand dollars for your service, whether the women win the money for their charity or not."

Ryker folded his arms across his chest and grinned. "Any rules against the woman falling in love with me?" He was the charmer and the flirt of the group with a mischievous grin, curly blond hair, bright blue eyes, and an innocent face women couldn't resist.

Emerald chuckled. "On the contrary, Mr. Sant, we welcome flirtations and some innocent physical contact." She winked. "Ups ratings, you see?"

Tanner groaned. "I'm out. I'm not dealing with some famous frou-frou woman wearing her high heels through the jungle and trying to flirt with and touch me." Tanner had been Dear John'ed a few months before he was released and was still bitter against women.

"Let it go," Tagg said. "She wasn't worthy of you anyway."

"I'm trying, man," Tanner muttered.

Ace nodded. "I'm with you, Tanner. I've got enough women coming on to me." He snuck a glance at Emerald again.

"Ooh," Ryker teased. "Big Dog's gotta fight them off with a stick!"

A few men hooted at that. Ace was always calling himself "Big Dog" usually when it was dinnertime and he was fighting for more than his share of the meal.

Brit smiled at the interaction. It didn't matter to him. He'd promised his life to the girl of his dreams when he was eighteen, sworn his life away on a Holy Bible. When she'd unexpectedly died two months later, she'd taken any chance of him ever finding love again to her grave.

Emerald's eyes widened, but she focused on Ace instead of Tanner, Tagg, or Ryker. "You don't have to flirt with or grow close to the woman. The show's direction will really be up to you and your female counterpart. I assure you there will be plenty of excitement without any romance, if you choose to keep your distance emotionally. Physically, you will have to be somewhat close. You're protecting them and if you have a tent, you'll only have one. That type of thing." She bit at her lip and looked away from Ace.

Ace looked like a deer in the headlights. Brit had to hide his smile. He was obviously being lured in by this competent woman's beautiful face and shape.

Kane and Satchel looked at each other and shrugged. Fifty thousand was a decent paycheck and they all liked adventure, but it was a wild card what the women would be like. For the most part, they weren't proficient at girl-speak—they'd spent the last decade or more with mostly tough and hardened men.

Who knew what kind of hot water they could get themselves into?

"I'm out," Tanner said. "If I go on a reality show I won't be able to do uncover jobs to fight trafficking anymore."

Emerald gave him a level look. "We're way ahead of you, Mr. McKay. Obfuscation software is available for any of you who would like your face obscured during the show."

"Perfect for plug-uglies like you." Ryker pushed at Tagg who shoved him back. They all laughed.

"I appreciate you thinking of that but t's not worth it," Tanner said. "Women and me are no bueno."

Emerald tilted her chin in a challenge and asked, "What would you do it for?"

Britton's heart picked up in speed. Apparently, whoever was funding this show really wanted him and his men. Maybe the producer would earn it back, but maybe not. "Who's your boss?" he asked before Tanner could answer.

Emerald shook her head and her face tightened. "I'm not at liberty to say."

Britton looked at the other men. They were starting to look uneasy. "How do we know he or she can be trusted to pay us? That they're not going to put us into some modern-day gladiator situation?"

"I will swear to you on a stack of Holy Bibles," Emerald began. "This job is legit. Yes, you will face obstacles and danger. Maybe the women will be hard to protect or work with, but it will be well worth it for you."

They all stared at her, obviously wanting more. For Brit it was enough; he was struggling with facing his future at this point anyway. A week of adventure and testing sounded much better than trying to find a death-defying job where he could risk his life and help others. He didn't want his men to needlessly risk themselves, but they were all strong, well-trained—by him—and more than up for any adventure.

"I can also promise you my boss is the best man I've ever known," Emerald continued. Ace's shoulders rounded at that statement and his eyes dimmed. "He's a billionaire who honors veterans and wanted to give you men the chance to earn a large paycheck. You can trust him, and you can trust me."

The room was silent for a moment. Tanner said, a little belligerently, "Sorry. It's just not that enticing to me."

"I need you all to commit or I have to find another group." Emerald looked a little weary at that prospect. "And unbeknownst to you, I've been researching all of you and the women you'll be paired with. I have put a lot of time and thought into this." She held up a hand before any of them could protest further. "Not that any of you should care about the time I've spent. I'm just saying that your adventures and your female counterparts would be a good match for each of you. Yes, it will be dangerous, but I thought you were all the type to laugh in the face of danger."

Ace poked out his chest. "I am."

Britton had to hide a smile. Her baiting would work for some, but Tanner still appeared uninterested.

"What's it going to take, Mr. McKay?" she swung on Tanner. "A hundred grand?"

Someone whistled and Ace called out, "Sign me up."

Emerald gave Ace a warm smile that brought the brightness back to his eyes. She looked back at Tanner. She must have had schooling on how to read people, because she seemed to quickly know he wasn't in yet. "Two hundred thousand?" she upped the ante.

"Please," Ace said to Tanner.

Tanner smiled at him, shaking his head. "I don't know, man."

"Five hundred thousand," Emerald said.

The room went dead silent. Even Tanner looked impressed. A few beats passed, then some of the men started muttering, some talking more loudly.

"I could start my restaurant on Vieques," Eli said.

"I could pay off my grandpa's farm," Satchel said.

"I could fight trafficking full time for a lot of years on half a million dollars," Tagg added.

They all nodded. Each of them had dreams and goals, charities or businesses they wanted to start, lives they wanted to lead. Everybody except Britton. Their leader, who now had no idea where he was going with his life. He loved supporting and working with a variety of causes, but he couldn't say any one of them was his life's calling. In the past twelve years, his men and his missions had distracted him from the emptiness of his future, but now that he was back home, it had hit him between the eyes. If only he dared confide in his trusted pastor about the impetuous vow he'd made at eighteen. The vow that now made it impossible for him to ever find love and have a family.

In the military, with his friends, life hadn't felt quite so empty.

Shaking the depressing thoughts off, he looked at his former team, now his friends. Half a million dollars would change their lives. Maybe this was exactly what he needed to move forward in a positive way. He'd never have love or a family of his own, but at least he could have a purpose. If he stepped forward, he knew they'd follow suit. It was what they'd been trained to do, but they also trusted him implicitly.

"I'm in," Britton said, stepping up next to Emerald and giving her a nod, then looking out over the team. He wanted to know exactly who her boss was. There was a chance it was his old high school teammate-turned-billionaire, but it didn't really matter at the moment. He and his buddies needed this.

Relief showed in the woman's blue eyes. She smiled her gratitude. "Your leader is in. What about the rest of you?"

Ace nodded eagerly, giving her a secretive smile that luckily only Britton and Emerald saw or the razzing would've been off the charts. Emerald's cheeks tinged pink.

Satchel and Kane nodded more reluctantly.

"It's intriguing," Denzel admitted. "I'll commit to one week for half a million dollars."

"Let's do this," Eli said.

"Let's go, boys!" Ryker hollered, flexing and letting out a whoop.

Emerald appeared amused as the rest of them chuckled. Everyone's eyes went to the last two holdouts. Tanner and Tagg looked at each other. They'd been best friends since college and were heavily involved in the anti-trafficking battle. It would be tough for them to take a break, but a week wasn't that long. Half a million dollars would give them the independence to commit more time and money to their causes.

"It is a smart move," Denzel said quietly to them.

Tagg nodded. "Let's do it."

Tanner put up his hands. "I want it known that I'm doing this for all of you, not for some unknown woman she's matched me up with."

Ryker bounded over to him and put him in a headlock, rubbing his hair as Tanner fought him off. "That's my boy. Always thinking of others."

Everyone laughed and started jostling each other. The room

was suddenly full of excitement and anticipation. Half a million dollars would be incredible, but the adventure could be a lot of fun too. The unknown called to them.

Britton felt a peace settle over him. Everyone was in, and he had a purpose again.

"Now," Emerald called and they settled a little bit, "each of you will have to commit to no contact with the media for the next six months until the shows have all aired."

They all shrugged and then nodded. What did they care about interviews and exposure?

"Thank you. You will also have to commit to no contact with each other for the next eight weeks," Emerald said, still smiling.

"What?" The room seemed to explode with that one question. Ryker released Tanner and joined in the calls of, "No way! We can't do that!"

Emerald's smile was replaced with a look of panic as she tried to talk over the noise. "Please, please."

"Listen to her," Ace hollered, but nobody was listening.

"Please," she tried to continue. "I know it will be rough because you're close friends, but with one of you having an adventure each week for the next eight weeks, we can't have you sharing information." She looked to Britton. "Please, help me explain to them."

"Team," Britton called sharply.

Everyone stopped talking and looked to him.

"You don't have to do this, but I think we all know what a difference we can each make with half a million dollars." He paused and looked at each of them in turn. "Eight weeks will go quickly and we'll be back together laughing about our adventures. Besides, after living with you savages for years, a break will help me fit in with civilized people." He smirked and waited for their response.

The other men's eyes moved from one to another as they carried on a non-verbal conversation they'd perfected through numerous missions.

Ace was the first to speak. "Well, Cap, you couldn't carry a tune even if you had a bucket."

"And he snores," added Tagg.

Denzel waved a dismissive hand. "You're picking on Cap? Don't get me started on how bad all of your feet smell after three days without changing socks. I'll gladly take eight weeks without smelling that."

Brit looked to Emerald as the teasing escalated for a few minutes. "We're still in. When do we start?"

Emerald smiled again. "The first week starts on Monday. Are you volunteering to go first, Mr. Grady?"

Britton gave his men what they'd dubbed his "make the devil cry" grin. "Of course I am. I'm the team leader."

As one, all seven of his men clapped and cheered. Britton's smile grew. Apparently, his words were all they needed to put their worries away. What was there to worry about? One week roughing it with a woman for half a million dollars.

Piece of cake.

CHAPTER ONE

Tess James shielded her eyes. The black asphalt reflected the sun and made it feel even hotter. It was April, for goodness sake, but somebody forgot to tell this fancy private airport east of Phoenix, Arizona. Sweat ran in rivulets down her back and pooled in her bra. She'd had her last shower for the week this morning and had at least planned on staying clean and nice-smelling until they reached whatever remote destination she and her military counterpart were supposed to conquer. Apparently not. If she kept this sweating up, she'd smell like a three-hundred-pound pro wrestler who never washed his stretchy pants.

She smiled to herself and the cameraman gave her a thumbs up. From what she understood, this segment of her first meeting with the military hero would be filmed, but then she'd be in charge of filming on the camera they would provide for the rest of the week. The filming would not be expert, but she had done enough filming of herself to promote her charity that she would do just fine. She only hoped she could get enough footage for the show as she scaled a mountain or swam with crocodiles or whatever they asked of her. She shivered with delight. She was going to get out and live. Oh! She was excited, and terrified. Maybe more terrified than excited.

A silver truck pulled into the small parking lot and a man climbed out. He straightened to his full height and looked her direction. Tess sucked in a breath and murmured, "Woo-ee, lucky me. I got the hot military hero."

He strode their direction, carrying nothing. They'd been instructed that the show would provide their bag of supplies and they were to bring nothing but the clothes on their back. He looked tough and irresistible and he had one of those walks that had ... purpose. He was large and in charge and it looked great on him. His hair was dark and cut short and his jaw line was manly and smooth. He had a high brow and his lips were a nice bow-shape, almost too-pretty, but nothing about this tough guy could be considered too-anything but perfectly appetizing.

His eyes zeroed in on her as he approached and she knew she'd found her favorite part of him. Those eyes were deep brown and framed with lashes she was jealous of. They were incredible.

"H-hey," she stuttered, lifting her hand and forgetting to shield her forehead. What woman cared about sun-damaged eyes when a man like this was looking at her?

He stepped right up and extended his hand. "Britton Grady. Nice to meet you, ma'am."

He even talked like a military man. "You too," she managed, clinging to his hand and giving it an extra-long shake. His hand was nice: manly, strong, perfect. She turned it over with her own hand and looked at the back of it, tanned with strong vein lines. Definitely her type of hand. "I like it," she said. As she looked up, she caught a flash of humor in his eyes, but it was there and gone quick. "Your hand," she clarified. "It's a good one."

He pulled his hand back, regretfully, and said, "And you are?"

"Oh!" She laughed and put her hand to her chest. "Tessannalisa Magdelana James. I guess my parents gave me impossibly long first and second names to make up for our lame, boring last name. And ... you don't care. You can call me Tess."

He actually gave her what she thought might be his full smile. It crinkled the edges of his eyes and mouth and, more importantly, lit up those beautiful dark eyes of his. His smile was as glorious as the rest of him. She swooned. At least in her mind. Luckily, she didn't fall over on the burning asphalt.

"Pleasure to meet you, Tess. How did they rope you into ... all of this?"

"Oh, it wasn't hard, *believe* me. I'm hopefully going to earn half a million dollars for my charity, Love the Littles. How generous and incredible is that?" His brows arched but he said nothing, so she kept talking, as was normal for her. "Plus, I got so excited about the whole adventure of it. I love Bear Grylls and Survivor and Amazing Race and you'll even catch me watching Naked and Afraid on occasion. Have you ever watched that? Wild. Absolutely insane. I love it all."

She'd never actually done anything adventurous. Would he want to ditch his assignment when he realized how domesticated she was? Her parents were the dentist and oral hygienist in her tiny town of Pine, Arizona. Everybody knew, loved, and protected her. Only the real rebels in town would've let her do brave stuff like balance on their fence posts or sneak her Halloween candy that "rotted her teeth out" according to her parents. As an adult, she had a stash of licorice that nobody knew about.

"Except for the eating yucky, disgusting stuff," she continued. "Are you good at killing in the wild, Hot Military Hero? Do you think they'll give us any food or you think we'll starve? I don't like being hungry, but I promise you won't hear me complain." His eyes widened as she driveled on. She took that as her cue to zip it. "I apologize. I tend to ramble when I'm nervous." She flapped her arms. "Sweating like a stuffed pig here. I'm from Pine, actual mountains and trees. Aren't you hot? You don't even look hot."

The cameraman chuckled, reminding Tess they weren't alone. She ducked her head in embarrassment, scared to meet Britton's gaze but unable to pull her eyes from him. He was so incredible. If she could stop her runaway tongue, this might be the best week of her life. It would definitely be the most excit-ing. She wouldn't know adventure if it bit her on the hind side. Even if she didn't humiliate herself with her lack of survival skills, would a guy like this actually notice an Average Ally like her? He would be stuck with her for a week. Maybe her shining personality would hook him. She grimaced. Or her flapping tongue would drive him insane. She mentally slapped herself. She needed to focus on the charity, not how to get Hot Military Man interested in her.

"I'm hot," he admitted, but he didn't look it in a fitted t-shirt, joggers, and running shoes. He looked model perfect. "What are you nervous about?"

Her eyes widened. "Everything! I love those adventure reality shows, but I actually have zero survival skills. Zilch!" She made a zero with her fingers and thumb and realized—dang, she'd admitted the truth to him before they were stuck in a cave with wolves outside. Would he run from her before the show started? She continued talking despite wondering if she should cut off her rambling tongue. "Will we die out there? Will we starve to death? Will cannibals eat us? Will I win the money and help untold children or will I fail and disappoint the entire world?" She threw a dramatic hand up. "Not to mention I'm alone with some unknown hottie for a week. What *don't* I have to be nervous about?"

His lips twitched but all he said was, "First, I can reassure you I will protect you and you are safe with me."

She fanned her face. "I'm going to swoon. I hope he catches this on film because you are going to have to catch me."

His face tightened with concern and he took a step closer, extending his hand. "Are you serious?"

She waited, trying to ascertain if she would indeed swoon, but then she deflated with disappointment. She'd read about it a lot, but it had never happened to her, not even close. But then, she'd never been close to a man like this. "Nope. Sorry. But thank you for being willing to catch me. That was awfully sweet of you." She batted her eyelashes at him.

"Of course." He studied her as if not certain if she was emotionally stable. She needed to button her mouth or he'd run before they even got on the airplane.

She took a breath and tried to redirect. An airplane was angling toward the runway. Was it theirs? "Do you think we'll parachute out of the airplane?"

He smiled and shook his head, pointing at the sleek white plane that was descending. "That's a Learjet 75. I doubt our eccentric billionaire will risk depressurizing the cabin to push us out with parachutes."

"Oh." She deflated again. The mental picture of them

strapped together, floating beautifully through the air, had been appealing. But they would have a lot of alone time and chances to grow close over the next week. She perked back up. "How do you know he's eccentric? Do you know the billionaire who put this all together?"

He shook his head. "Forgive me. I don't know that. I only assumed anyone willing to spend millions of dollars on an untested reality TV show that may or may not give him a return on that investment must be somewhat ... eccentric." He glanced uneasily at the camera, obviously not wanting to badmouth their benefactor.

"But it's not millions. I mean, even if I win, I only get half a million for my charity. I mean, *not* 'only.' It's very generous and will be absolutely incredible. I'm just saying, it isn't millions."

He shifted from foot to foot and then cleared his throat. "You do realize there are seven other couples who will be doing their own weeklong shows?"

"No kidding? Oh, that's cool. I'd love to hear what the other charities are. I guess that could add up to millions." She looked him over. "What do you get out of this, besides the publicity of being awesome, helping my charity, and saving my thick neck when I run straight off a cliff or something?" She grinned.

"I'm not doing it for publicity," he murmured.

The plane had landed as she talked and now it taxied up close to them. Britton focused on it. The door descended, transforming into steps, and a man climbed out. He was a polished, handsome type of dude with perfectly tousled golden brown hair, the perfect five o'clock shadow, the perfectly-handsome face, and the perfectly-toned body. He had on sunglasses and a tailored suit. His smile grew as he approached them.

He looked a little too perfect for Tess's taste, but that could just be her inner introvert who'd never interacted with the likes of either of these two men. She found herself easing a little closer to her studly military hero. Britton stared at the man with a glint in his eye and a smirk on his lips.

Their billionaire took his glasses off and extended his hand to her first. "Miss James. Thank you for being here. Your charity, Love the Littles, and your inspirational thoughts on social media have uplifted me. My executive assistant is a huge fan of yours and bemoaning the fact she can't meet you today. Thank you for what you do for the children."

Her brow squiggled and she thought she really might swoon. "You're ..." She knew exactly who he was but for once her tongue failed her.

"Axel Dexter," he supplied, grinning at her. "Pleasure to have you be part of the show, Miss James."

Axel Dexter followed her on social media ... no! She had hundreds of thousands of followers, but she would've noticed that name.

He turned to Britton and opened his arms. "Brit!"

Tess's jaw dropped as they grabbed each other in one of those manly backslapping hugs and kept on backslapping and laughing. Tess simply stared. Axel Dexter—billionaire, philanthropist, former Army Ranger, only son of a Texas oil tycoon. He was one of the most impressive men of their day. She had shaken his hand and was now staring at him hugging her military protector. Even his critics couldn't find anything to fault about Axel Dexter, except for the fact that his money was family money, but he'd been raised by a single mom in a poor area of Dallas. He'd only received his fortune when the father he'd never met died of a heart attack two years ago. It was hard for anybody to claim he'd been born with a silver spoon in his mouth.

She looked at her hand; she would never wash it again. A laugh bubbled out of her. She wouldn't be washing it for a week, that was for certain.

The men finally pulled apart and turned to her. She stopped laughing.

"Forgive us," Axel said smoothly. "We haven't seen each other in years." He put his hand on Britton's arm. "This guy was the stud of our high school. Took Cedar Hills to two state championship wins."

Britton was smiling bigger than Tess had thought possible. "Only because you caught—" Britton paused and seemed to calculate in his head "—at least twenty percent of the passes I threw to you."

"Oh-ho!" Axel laughed. "That's because you had terrible aim." He gave Tess a conspiratorial look. "But he was big enough and fast enough that he could run through anybody's defensive line."

Britton only smiled at his praise. "Sometimes it seems like yesterday."

Axel nodded, his expression turning a little more serious. "A lot of life between then and now, though."

Britton's smile fled. "For sure. You look great, man. Congrats on all your success."

"Ah, it's easy when your daddy, who you never knew existed, dies and hands it all to you. Just ask my critics." He winked at Tess. She hadn't known he had critics but she supposed everyone who put themselves in the public eye would at one time or another.

Britton shook his head. "I know that's a lie. I remember what a hard worker you always were." He looked to Tess. "Coach would demand extra sprints at the end of an incredibly hard practice and this guy would push himself till he puked. He was so fast nobody could catch him at practice or in games."

"Gross, the puking part," she said. "And impressive, the hard-working part." She worked hard on her charity and she did yoga and took long walks every day. Running until she puked? Nope. Never.

"Impressive," Britton said.

Things went quiet for a half a beat as if Axel was embarrassed by that revelation while the cameras rolled. He looked into Britton's eyes and said quietly, "I was so sorry to hear about ..." His eyes cut to Tess. "Your loss."

Now Britton was the one looking tense and awkward and Tess was going absolutely nuts wondering who he had lost. Did her amazing military man have a tragic story and a broken heart? It made her want to cry. She only wanted happiness for this tough, appealing man.

"Thank you," Britton said.

A tense silence ensued.

Britton cleared his throat. "I wondered if it was you behind this idea when some gorgeous 'personal assistant' gathered my men and made us an offer that we couldn't refuse."

Tess's brow squiggled. Gorgeous girl? Offer? Her military hero wasn't just here to help her?

"Why didn't you just ask me?" Britton asked, pointing from the cameraman to Tess, obviously confused why his friend would involve him in some setup.

"What would be the fun in that?" Axel's grin was back. "You remember how I love drama."

"Do I ever." Britton rolled his eyes.

"Ah, c'mon, you're not still mad Jessica chose me, are you?" Axel leaned closer to Tess. "Junior year. The Homecoming

Queen was a year older than us. Jessica Lee Vulture." He drew
the name out like it was hot fudge sauce.

"Her name wasn't really Vulture," Tess protested. These two
were so much fun to be around. Were all men like this? She
wouldn't know. The only men near her age in her hometown
were nice boys, but they were as awkward around her as she
probably was around them. They spent most of their free time
tipping cows and racing their trucks up mountains.

"It was." Axel's blue eyes sparkled and she wasn't sure what
to believe. "I snaked her from Brit and he's never forgiven me."

Britton's face was serious, giving nothing away.

"I saved you a whole lot of drama," Axel promised, slapping
Britton on the shoulder and then making a crazy symbol with his
hand swirling by his ear. "Well." Axel rubbed his hands together.
"I need to let you two be on your way. You take my jet. I'll take
your rental and go enjoy Phoenix until my pilot comes back. I'll
see you Saturday."

Tess felt her stomach plunge. This was it. They were on their
way. "What are our rules and instructions?"

Axel waved a hand. "No stress, no rules." He beamed at the
two of them. "You two have six days to discover a secret treasure. It is located within one mile of your drop zone."

"So it's buried within a mile of where you drop us?" Her brow
wrinkled.

"Maybe buried, maybe hidden in a tree, maybe hidden in a
waterfall, maybe hidden in plain sight." He winked. "You've got a
week to figure it out and win a half a million for your charity."
He lowered his voice. "And just between you and I, Tess, I gave
you the best man I know to protect and help you."

Tess's gaze cut to Britton. He looked uncomfortable with the
praise. She got warm all over thinking about spending a week

with this guy. She'd braced herself for *Survivor*, but it sounded like they were going on a fun treasure hunt. They could explore a mile in every direction easily in a week's time. She wondered where they were going. He'd mentioned waterfalls and trees ... ooh, she would bet it was going to be beautiful. This was going to be incredible.

"Thank you," she managed.

Axel turned and walked to the plane and they fell into step with him. "The pilot will take your cell phones before you transfer to the helicopter and he'll give you the cameras. You'll set up stationary cameras at base camp that will run twenty-four hours. Please wear the GoPro every time you leave camp, extra batteries will be in your day pack. Brit will have a satellite phone for any emergencies or to call when you find the prize early." He winked. They stopped outside the door to the plane and he turned to Britton. "I picked you and your team because I know how good *you* are and I'm trusting you trained them to be almost as good."

Britton nodded very seriously.

"There will be no predators where you are going, but the terrain is dangerous and you may encounter some ... interesting locals, maybe severe weather, so please stay safe." Tess's stomach swooped again. Axel tilted his head to her. "Keep her safe."

Britton stared into her eyes and she wondered if she'd swoon for real this time. "I will protect her." He said the words as if they were a promise. He'd keep her safe. He'd protect her with his life. She felt like a princess in medieval times and she was grateful Axel had given her his top knight.

Axel shook her hand warmly again, gave Britton one more side hug, and then stepped back.

Tess walked up the few steps into the plane, gawking at the

luxurious tan leather seats. Britton followed her in. She turned to him and mouthed, "Wow!"

He smiled.

She heard voices outside the plane and then an older gentleman walked in, closing the door behind him. "Miss James, Mr. Grady. Pleasure to meet you both. George Sinclair, at your service. I'll be flying you to Kauai to meet your helicopter pilot." He must've exited the plane while they were talking and she hadn't even noticed.

"Kauai?" Tess squealed and clapped her hands together. "This just gets better and better!"

Mr. Sinclair smiled and then excused himself and walked to the cockpit. He turned at the open door. "Please feel free to sit anywhere you'd like. There are drinks and refreshments in the fridge and cupboard." He gestured toward the back of the plane. "And a restroom for your use. If you'll just please buckle in for takeoff and landing, you're free to roam any other time, unless we hit turbulence."

"Thank you," Britton said.

Mr. Sinclair lifted a hand and disappeared into the cockpit.

Tess sank into the closest leather chair with a sigh. "I think I'm in heaven."

Britton smiled and sat across the aisle from her. "Enjoy it. I have a feeling things will get a little rough for us when we get to Kauai."

Tess straightened. "What do you mean? Mr. Billionaire Hottie is your buddy. He wouldn't put you in a tough situation. We have a week to find a treasure. Should be a piece of double chocolate cake with cream cheese icing with my tough military hero along."

Britton's eyebrows lifted. "Axel's a great guy and a friend from high school, but he isn't going to make this easy on us. He was dead serious about me keeping you safe. We both signed and agreed to be here at our own risk, including the possibility of death or disability. He doesn't want us to die on his show, but it's a possibility."

She leaned away from him. "Die? It's Kauai. It's paradise."

Britton reclined into his chair and put his seatbelt on. "I've vowed to keep you safe, Miss James. I will do so, but please take the danger of this week seriously."

"Um ... okay," she squeaked out. For once, she couldn't think of anything else to say. The plane started to taxi toward the short runway. "Can you please call me Tess?"

He gave her a fleeting smile. "Tess."

Her stomach warmed. She loved the way her name rolled off his lips. They might be going into danger, but with this guy, she couldn't bring herself to worry much. He was like Bear Grylls, Crocodile Dundee, and Captain America rolled into one. "Can I call you Brit like Axel did?"

"Sure."

They shared a smile as the plane lifted smoothly into the air.

"Crap!" she cried out. "I didn't even have time to be scared."

Brit chuckled. "I hope you say that a lot this week."

Tess bit her lip. She hoped she wasn't scared at all. Was she really up for this adventure? It was to help the children and expand her charity like she'd never dreamt she could do. She'd remember her focus, and they would find that darn treasure.

Now if only she could stop staring at her protector. To her, he was more handsome than even the charismatic billionaire heart-throb Axel Dexter.

CHAPTER TWO

B ritton waited for Tess's motor mouth to start up again as the plane flew to the west, but she busied herself on her phone, probably dealing with emails and whatever she needed to shut down for the next week while she was gone. She took a short video talking to her "friends" and telling them goodbye. She panned to Brit and he simply waved, smiled, and said hello. It was awkward. He wasn't active on social media and had never taken a selfie video. Besides sending a few goodbye texts to his parents, sister, and some friends, and then Googling tips on survival in Kauai's jungle and on treasure hunting, he didn't know what to do with his phone besides read scriptures on it while Tess worked. He would miss his scripture reading for the next week. The good word gave him more peace than anything else ever had, but the instructions had said to bring nothing but his phone, which he would leave with the pilot when they got there.

He wondered if he should've revealed to Tess that he was

getting paid half a million dollars regardless of if they found the "treasure." At some point he would. He could just imagine all she'd have to say about that.

It was just like the Axel he remembered from high school to not come directly to him and simply ask Brit if he could hire his men. If Brit would've known it was Axel, he would've talked his men into doing the gig for a simple fee, nowhere close to half a million dollars each. Maybe that's why Axel had done it this way —because he wanted them to have the money. Even before Axel had received his unknown inheritance, he'd been the most generous of their group, always buying lunch or signing his buddies up for service projects. Brit would always love his friend from middle school on up. Nobody, not even Axel, knew back then that his dad was a billionaire oil tycoon. Brit was happy for Axel's success and impressed but not surprised that his friend was using that money to help charities, and help Brit's men. Having served in the military himself, Axel probably knew first-hand how much Britton's guys had sacrificed. He wondered what generosity Axel had bestowed on his own squadron.

He smiled to himself as he thought of Axel's teasing. Jessica Vulture. Ha. Brit couldn't even remember her real last name. Axel definitely had gotten the short end of the stick dating her.

It felt good to think about happier times, before the horrors of the military, seeing men, women, and children killed and before ...

As always, Kelley's beautiful face and big brown eyes played through his mind. She'd been his second choice for Home-coming their junior year, but halfway through the date, he'd been head over heels. They'd been inseparable throughout the last two years of high school. When he'd come home from basic training and before he left to go fulltime into the Navy, she'd made him a solemn, desperate, heartfelt vow. If he died, she would never love again and would live her life alone. He'd tried to talk her out of it, knowing he may very well die, but she'd been adamant and obstinate. He'd felt he had no choice but to return the promise—if something happened to her, he'd never love again. It had been easy for him to make that vow, even though he hadn't wanted her to commit to it and live without love. Neither one of them could've imagined she'd be the one to die and he'd survive … alone.

He closed his eyes and tried to push the once painful but now frustrating memories away. He needed to focus on the present, envision what the next week might look like. Axel wouldn't try to hurt anyone directly, especially Brit, but there wouldn't be any excitement to the show if they easily found the treasure with no risk involved. He hoped the bubbly brunette seated next to him realized what she was getting herself into. He seriously doubted she'd ever done anything more dangerous than mow her lawn.

He snuck a peek at her and found himself smiling. His protection detail was … adorable. Yeah, that was the best word to describe her. She had a curvy shape, curly reddish-brown hair, a perky nose, full cheeks with deep dimples when she smiled, and pretty rosebud lips. He really liked her eyes. They were an aqua green color with thick lashes. They lit up as she ran that motor mouth of hers. If she was one of his men, he'd already have asked for more work and less talk, but he enjoyed listening to her ramble—and she definitely wasn't one of his men. He hoped he'd responded appropriately to her so far.

He closed his eyes again. This type of protection detail wouldn't be a hardship for him, but he really hoped looking *after* her wouldn't be a nightmare. He wanted to keep her far from danger. She looked and sounded far too innocent to have any type of real-world experience. She'd already admitted she loved adventure reality shows but had never done anything adventurous herself.

At least there was no danger of him falling in love with her, no matter how appealing she might be. His heart was locked and no matter how many times his mom, sister, or pastor begged him to forget about Kelley and move on, he couldn't do it. He couldn't go back on a promise that only he, Kelley, and the angels in heaven knew about. The innocent teenage love he'd had for Kelley had faded almost completely, but he was bound by his word and he had no idea how to change that. For a lot of years, busy with his military career and assignments, he hadn't cared much to change it. Now his future stretched ahead of him, empty and alone.

Brit was naturally quiet and he liked hearing Tess talk. Hopefully, once she finished whatever she was doing on her phone, she'd start chatting again.

He folded his arms across his chest and tilted his head to the side. These seats were comfortable. Might as well enjoy it now, because he knew what the next week might entail and a comfortable seat wasn't in the cards. He felt himself drifting off and let himself enjoy having nothing to do for a few minutes.

"Brit, Brit." A warm hand was on his arm. "We're here."

Brit straightened and swiped a hand over his face. "Sorry, I drifted off."

"No stress." She gave him a smile and her dimples deepened. "We might not be sleeping much the next week." She winked at him and his heart started racing. Did she mean ...? An image rose unbidden. Brit holding her in his arms while they kissed the night away and definitely didn't sleep. Whoa. He hadn't let his mind stray like that in years. Holding Tess was nowhere in the job description. Absolutely not. Over the past twelve years since losing Kelley, he'd fallen to peer pressure—or mom or sister pressure—when he was home on leave and had gone on a few dates. It had meant nothing to him; his promise to Kelley had never left the forefront of his mind. How on earth had this pipsqueak of a beautiful, talkative woman caused him to have weird fantasies so quick?

The plane descended and she gripped her armrests as they bumped once on the tarmac and then settled. The pilot hit the brakes. She pulled in a quick breath.

"Are you okay?" he asked.

She gave him a shaky smile. "Not a big flyer," she admitted. "Excuse me for a second while I say a prayer of gratitude." She bowed her head and he watched her lips move as she prayed. She really was far too cute. He prayed, but not over every little thing. As innocent and appealing as she was, he'd need to be extra careful not to get emotionally invested.

That might prove tougher than protecting her and finding whatever elusive treasure Axel had hidden. Knowing his friend, he'd hidden it personally.

The plane taxied to a stop and she lifted her head, giving him an irresistible smile. "On to adventure, my brave military hero." She punched a fist in the air.

He chuckled. He wouldn't let himself fall in love—of course he wouldn't—but there was no reason he couldn't enjoy being around her. He could make a new friend, maybe even try to think of her like a little sister.

His gaze caught on her lips. That might be tough to do.

"Why do you sound like you're marching to the executioner's chair?" he asked.

She lifted her shoulders. "I can admit the truth to you, now that you're stuck with me." She winked and he wondered if she realized she'd already told him she only watched adventure on the television. "I'm a complete wuss, have never camped in my life, and I'm less of an adventurer than Scarlett O'Hara, but how could I possibly resist when offered a half a million dollars for Love the Littles?"

He wanted to reassure her that she would be fine, but he also wanted to ask her about her charity. Before he could do either, the pilot exited the cockpit, asked them how their flight was, and then escorted them from the plane. He conferred with a couple of large men who were waiting nearby and the men started unloading boxes from the cargo hold.

Maybe they wouldn't be eating squirrel and snake the next week. Oh, wait; no snakes on Kauai. That was one small blessing.

George extended his hand. "Time to turn over those phones."

They both put their cell phones in his hand.

"I promise I will keep them safe." He handed Brit the satellite phone, then handed over several bags to Tess. "You're in charge of setting up all the cameras at your base camp and carrying extra batteries in your backpack for the GoPro." He inclined his head to a helicopter where the men were loading four boxes and a couple of backpacks. "The rest of your supplies are with the helicopter. I think you're one of the lucky couples. You can establish a base camp instead of having to be on the move and living out of a backpack for a week."

Brit nodded. He wouldn't mind having food, a tent, and maybe even a pillow, but who knew what would be in those boxes? With Axel, he couldn't be certain. The man had been king of pranks on their high school football team. They'd both grown up a lot since then.

It would be nice, though, if he didn't have to spend too much time setting up a shelter or scavenging for food. Brit knew how thick the jungles and forested sections of Kauai were. They wouldn't make quick progress through a mile in each direction. "Thank you."

They each shook the man's hand and then walked to the helicopter.

A couple burly-looking locals grinned at them. "Hey, brah. What's up, *malihini?*" The men each gave Brit a fist bump.

"*Malihini?*" Tess's brow wrinkled.

"It means you be a non-native, *wahine nani,*" the other man said.

"Now what on earth does *waha-nana* ... or whatever that was, mean?"

The guy chuckled. "I'm Joe, pretty girl, and *wahine nani* means ... beautiful woman." He gave her a broad wink and a long once-over.

Brit knew the men meant no harm, but he found his spine stiffening. Joe was big, and none of it was spare fat, but as Tess's protector he would keep her safe, even from Axel's helicopter pilot and assistant if needed.

Tess laughed. "You're one crazy man. How do I say that?"

Joe threw back his head and laughed. "Just call me *lolo.*"

"Perfect."

Brit relaxed. Tess was just naturally happy and attractive. Of course this man responded to that.

Joe and Kaleo escorted them to the helicopter. Kaleo sat in the pilot's seat and gestured to Brit. "You wanna sit shotgun, brah?" Kaleo yelled to be heard over the rotors.

Brit would've preferred to stay close to Tess, but he didn't make a fuss. These were Axel's men. They wouldn't push past harmless flirtations and it wasn't a big deal for some guy to sit in a helicopter by her. Brit hardly knew Tess; he wasn't sure why he was being so overprotective of her. He was supposed to protect her physically, but if she wanted to tease with some burly guy, that was her choice.

Joe obnoxiously helped Tess buckle up her seatbelt and then helped her put her headset on. Brit cringed but forced himself to stand down. If Tess looked the slightest bit uncomfortable, he would say something—or twist the guy into a pretzel. Brit put on the headset Kaleo handed to him. Half a minute later, they lifted off. Their headsets muffled the outside noise and only turned on when somebody spoke.

Joe alternated between bragging about how he was in the pro circuit surfing, and acting as Tess's personal tour guide. He gave Tess all kinds of history about the Hawaiian islands and his people and pointed out Uluwehi Falls and Opaeka'a Falls as they flew over each of them. They glided over incredible jungles and peaks. They turned south and Kaleo winked back at Tess. "Had to show you some tourist sites before we took you to your private oasis."

"Thank you," Tess exclaimed, clapping her hands together and looking so incredibly appealing. Brit hoped he could keep his head on straight this week. "This is the most beautiful spot in the world!"

Joe and Kaleo both laughed. "Just you wait, my *nani*." Joe patted her knee and Brit's back stiffened.

Tess appeared oblivious, exclaiming over and over again about everything from the flowering trees to a towering, green mountain to a stream cutting through it all. Kaleo was an excellent pilot; he'd fly down low into a valley then swoop up over the peaks. Tess would cry out in excitement bordering on fear each time he dipped or swooped, but she never stopped talking about the beauty of the place.

"Here it is," Joe said over the mic as they flew close to a picturesque waterfall. "Home sweet home for you two the next week. You're a lucky man, brah." He slapped Brit on the shoulder.

Brit tensed.

"I'm the lucky one," Tess gushed. "This is incredible. Oh, my, that's gorgeous, but ... oh wow, how are we going to get through that jungle a mile in each direction?"

Brit couldn't help but smile. She was finally seeing what they were in for. They would be able to navigate it, but it wouldn't be an easy walk through the woods and they wouldn't be able to see very far in any direction.

"Manawaiopuna Falls," Joe informed them. "Most people call them Jurassic Park Falls 'cause they used them in the first movie."

"Oh, that's right," Tess exclaimed. "I'm on a movie set. These falls are so much cooler in person."

They all laughed. What man could help but fall for Tess's charm? Wait ... Brit couldn't. He'd have to maintain some barriers this week. She was far too appealing to him already.

They set down on a designated helicopter pad close to the waterfall pool. Kaleo cut the rotors and Brit took off his headset and handed it over. They all climbed out and simply stared up at the cascading falls for a bit. It was incredible.

Kaleo broke the spell and got down to business. "Only way in or out of here is helicopter. Mr. Dexter got special permission for ya to stay a week. This is private property, so be careful as you're exploring not to rip anything apart."

Brit nodded, cringing inside. A machete would be the easiest way to get through the thick vegetation.

"Helicopter tours come in here a few times a day if there's good visibility, so I'd set up your camp in the trees a bit down the stream for some privacy. That way, nobody messes with your stuff while you're out exploring." Kaleo tilted his head to the waterfall. "Most people just check out the falls and take pics since they can only stay for twenty minutes. The water's good to drink. You're not supposed to swim in the pool, but if you need a bath, just wait until the tours are done in the evening and the owner said you're okay to float for a bit if you don't use soap. I don't think you have any soap in your supplies anyway." He smiled. "Any questions?"

Brit shook his head, glancing at Tess. Her eyes were wide as if she was just trying to take it all in. Her tongue was amazingly silent.

Joe grabbed a box and they all went to help unload the supplies. There were four large boxes and two backpacks. Joe balanced a huge box on each bicep, making Tess laugh and clap with delight. Brit resisted the urge to show her he could do the same. He and Kaleo each took a box as she carried the two backpacks.

They walked down the river a little bit until they found an opening and then pushed through the trees and low-hanging branches and vines. Kaleo gestured to a semi-cleared spot. "Pretty level. You could set up here and only have to clear a bit of brush and rocks."

"Thanks," Brit said.

"Oh, crap," Tess exclaimed. "I'm supposed to be videoing!"

Brit had forgotten as well. That would be a pain.

"You'd definitely better get a video of me." Joe gave her a wink and a smile.

Tess laughed and pulled out one of the cameras while Brit moved the boxes around and started opening them. He listened to Tess talking into the screen, introducing Joe and Kaleo and walking back up the side of the stream a bit to show off the incredible waterfall and setting.

"And this is my protector, military hero and all-around stud, Britton Grady. Wave, my friend," Tess instructed.

Brit gave her a wave and a smile.

"Tell us something inspiring."

Brit shook his head. His mind was busy. How were they going to search thoroughly through this jungle a mile in each direction? Not to mention, he felt awkward on camera. He'd have to get used to that. "Sorry, I've got nothing."

Tess looked disappointed, but she gave him an encouraging smile and then turned to Joe and Kaleo, who seemed more than happy to chat with her. Brit found a shovel and started clearing away a spot to set up the tent.

When Tess finished videoing, Joe and Kaleo came over and each shook his hand. "Sorry we can't stay to help, but our instructions are to leave you two alone." Joe winked and repeated, "Lucky man." He turned to Tess. "We'll come check on you if we have tours stop here."

"Sounds good." She tucked a curl behind one ear and grinned. "Thanks for all your help."

"Anytime ... anytime," Joe sad in a low, suggestive tone.

Brit felt his shoulders tense again and he took a step forward. It wasn't personal, but he would protect his assignment.

"Chance 'em, brah," Kaleo said to Brit, giving him a look that said he knew exactly what Brit was thinking, had seen the odd flash of jealousy that had raced through him.

Brit shook his head, coming back to reality. "Not happening. Thanks for the ride."

"Ah, don't miss out on the best part of life." The large native slammed his hand against Britton's shoulder, chuckled, and then walked away.

Brit's insides chilled. The best part of life had left this world twelve years ago. It was the last thing he'd wanted to happen, but he had to live with it. He glanced at the beautiful Tess. A fun, bright, happy woman like her could be the best part of some man's life, but not his.

Joe gave Tess one more lingering look before lifting his hand and following his friend.

"What did *that* mean?" Tess asked. "*Chance 'em, brah?*"

Brit shrugged. "Just take a chance. Referring to our adventure, I'm sure."

"Hmm." She lifted her eyebrows but set up the camera on its tripod and then turned to him, rubbing her hands together. "I'll get more cameras set up in a bit, but what have we got here? Did they stash any chocolate or candy for me?"

He laughed. She was really cute. "Let's look through it all and see."

When she came up close and brushed against his arm as she looked at the supplies, he wondered how he'd stay impervious to her charms for an entire week. He had to remember his promise to Kelley and keep his distance emotionally. Falling in love with this beautiful woman wasn't in the cards for him.

CHAPTER THREE

Tess had to stay focused, somehow find whatever "treasure" Axel had hidden, and help many more children than she ever thought possible, but there was so stinking much to be distracted by. The absolutely gorgeous scenery and breathtaking waterfall were crazily enough only a backdrop to the absolutely gorgeous and breathtaking man she got to spend the next six days with.

He was miles out of her league and probably dated super models and actresses when he wasn't out saving the world. But somehow, he seemed unbothered by her flapping tongue and she could've sworn she saw a flicker of jealousy in his gaze when she'd been chatting with the cool Hawaiian dude. She'd probably imagined it. He was professional and kind, but he'd kept his distance, definitely not flirting with her like the cute Joe had. It was a bummer to be sure, but she couldn't help but be drawn to the serious, tough military hero. He could easily be the zen to her zang. Balance out her impetuousness and her motor mouth.

She shook her head, doubting he'd let down his guard around her this week.

They'd unloaded and organized all the supplies. He'd helped her mount the stationary cameras in various spots and then they'd put up a small tent, which had sent her mind wandering to the idea of cuddling with her brawny military man. Yes, sleeping would definitely be ... interesting. Thankfully, they wouldn't be sleeping with creepy-crawlies scurrying over their faces. There were even two pillows, thin, inflatable pads, and two blankets. There was also a bucket packed with a one-week food supply—Brit had said the brand was the highest quality available for pre-packaged meals—and a small box filled with trail mix, protein bars, jerky, dried fruit, and even some hard candy.

"Is this good enough for your sweet tooth?" Brit asked lightly, a teasing note in his voice.

She put a hand on her hip and flipped her hair. "Well, it isn't licorice, but I guess it'll do in our extreme conditions." She winked and he chuckled. She felt warm all over; she liked making him laugh. He seemed much more relaxed now that Joe and Kaleo were gone. She wondered why.

They stacked everything next to the tent. Since it was all sealed packages, Brit said it should be fine. The backpacks also had hiking type foods and filtration water bottles along with small shovels, knives, and a rain poncho for each of them.

The rest of the supplies consisted of dry clothes, towels, a couple of camp chairs, matches, the satellite phone in case they got in trouble, and they even found a pack of playing cards.

When they'd gotten everything set up and organized and their little camp spot was ready, Tess stood back and clapped her hands together. "This is seriously so much better than what I imagined we'd have. I thought we'd be starting a fire with a stick and killing pigs to survive. Axel must feel really guilty about stealing that Vulture girl back in high school."

Brit gave her a patient smile that didn't crinkle his cheek or make his eyes light up. "I doubt it. I think they made it easier because we've only got six days to find some treasure a mile in each direction, through this." He gestured with his arm at the thick, impassable-looking jungle and mountains surrounding them.

"Sheesh! Rain on my optimistic fantasies, will you?" She winked at him. "What time is it? I feel naked without my phone. Is that lame of me or what?"

He looked her over and swallowed hard and then looked at his watch. "It's five."

"Oh, criminy! We've wasted almost an entire day. When I first heard about this, I was excited that it was Monday to Saturday so I wouldn't miss the Sabbath. I mean, I'm still happy about that, but now we've got like five days to find that treasure. Let's go!" She grabbed a backpack and swung it on, pulling out the GoPro camera and mounting it on the special attachment that went around her head. She probably looked goofy, but it was all part of the gig. "Which direction first, boss?"

He smiled at her—a patronizing, *you're a cute little girl* kind of smile. She should've taken offense, but she deserved it. She was so far out of her league, not just with him but with this entire adventure. He reached for the other backpack and then looked at his watch. "I can program this to know when we've gone a mile. It's a lot of area to explore. You're right; we should get going tonight while we have light, but then we need to sit down and form a plan. Let's try the easiest route tonight, down the creek."

"Oh yeah, a plan." She grinned. "That all sounds good." She

touched his arm and he kind of jolted. She really liked the feel of his firm flesh under her fingers. "Thanks for being here with me. I'd be a mess without you."

He nodded and she wondered if he thought she was a mess regardless. "I'll lead the way," was all he said.

She pasted on a bright, optimistic smile and followed his broad shoulders along the riverbank to the ... maybe south? Oh, goodness, she'd be in trouble without him. She tried to peel her eyes and search high and low for treasure, something in a tree, or maybe a spot of ground that looked like somebody had dug, or something glittering under the merry creek they walked by. It was hard not to focus on Brit's broad shoulders in front of her, or the ground to make sure she wouldn't trip and sprain an ankle or something. That would be a tragedy.

She wanted to talk to Brit, ask him question after question, but she stayed silent. They'd have all night in that tent to talk. A delicious shiver rippled through her. What would they do all alone after the sun went down? Her stomach rumbled. They should've both eaten on the plane. He'd been sleeping and she'd watched him sleep while she checked on all the social media and website posts for when she was gone, delivery of the weekend backpack meals for kids in need, teachers to cover her parenting and gardening classes, and a hundred other things that she'd prescheduled but wanted to check over and over again. She'd gone on close-by weekend vacations since she started her charity, but she'd never been without internet for a week.

"Are you hungry?" he asked over his shoulder.

She started. "Oh, you heard that too? I think it was actually a moose rumbling off in the woods, not my stomach."

He chuckled. "I don't believe there are any moose on the island."

"Dang, no excuse for my rumbling belly. Yes, I'm starving, but I promised you I wouldn't complain. How far have we gone?"

He checked his watch then turned back to her. "About a quarter of a mile."

"What?" She was stunned. They'd moved slowly; it wasn't an easy walking trail, and they didn't want to miss the treasure, but they couldn't be going that slow. That was crawling speed. "We are walking way too slow!"

He shrugged. "I don't want to miss anything."

"I'm with you. Dang. Are we even going to make it a mile and back before dark?"

"I don't know. Do you want to stop and eat?"

"Nope. We can eat when we're dead."

He looked at her strangely, the corner of his mouth turning up. "When we're dead?"

She laughed. "Sorry. Twisting one of my mom's expressions. She's a busy bee worker and Dad is always trying to get her to slow down. Her response is always, 'I'll sleep when I'm dead.'" Her mom had helped her start her charity and that hard work had made all the difference.

He smiled. "Okay, we'll eat when it's dark outside and we can't explore."

"Exactly." She clapped her hands together. "Let's soldier on, my soldier."

His smile grew brighter, then quickly flickered and died. Should she not have called him "my soldier?"

"Let's do it." He turned, picking up their slow pace. She tried to focus harder so she wouldn't miss a single clue. A mile in each direction hadn't sounded unreasonable back in Arizona. Even in Pine where she lived, there were trees, but it wasn't thick jungle like this and you could see a good distance in any direction.

A mile in this mess was getting more and more out of reach, especially if this path along the river—or creek, as it were—was the easiest path they would take. She glanced over her shoulder to where the waterfall towered. A mile climbing up that would be impossible. Finding a treasure didn't sound as easy as it had originally.

What would the other seven couples be doing during their weeks? So interesting that Axel Dexter had schemed this all up. Had he done it to be charitable with all his money or for more exposure? Maybe he was just bored. After a while, all that money would have to lose its shine. Then there'd be the endless questions of who you could trust. Maybe he'd done everything fun in the world and now he was bored. Maybe. She'd never know, but she didn't really care to experience piles of money. She was happy with her future, especially if she could win five-hundred-thousand and help even more children.

The creek babbled alongside them. She heard birds and insects singing, but otherwise it was just their footfalls and breathing. The helicopter tours must come in the morning; they hadn't seen any since Joe and Kaleo left.

"What happened to that busy tongue of yours?" Brit asked, surprising her out of her thoughts.

"What do you mean?"

"My first impression of you was that you wouldn't stop talking all week."

"Ouch," she mumbled. "I'm not trying to annoy you."

He stopped and turned to face her. The sun was getting lower and filtered through the tall trees. She liked the way it played with the shadows of his handsome face. "You aren't annoying. I like hearing you talk."

"Seriously?" Even her parents sometimes got tired of hearing her talk.

He nodded. "Talk away ... if you want to."

She wanted to ask him a million questions. First of all, who had Axel been referring to as "his loss?" Instead, she started with the basics. "Tell me about you. Where are you from? Oh, wait, Texas like Axel, right? Cedar Hills?"

"Yeah, that's right."

"So you played football—quarterback, right? You were the stud of the high school. You and Axel. I can just imagine it." She checked to make sure the camera was rolling. The viewers would be just as intrigued by Brit as she was. Well, maybe not quite as much. Even with all the shows she'd watched, she'd never known a real man could be this appealing.

Brit grunted and said, "I was hoping you'd talk about you, not me."

"But you're much more fun. So tell me all. Start with your family, please." Though she would've preferred starting with his dating history—past, present, and were there any future openings?

He blew out a long-suffering breath and said, "Not much to tell. Two parents, one sister. My family home is close to Joe Pool Lake, so whenever I wasn't playing football, we were boating. My sister and I both love the water."

"Oh, that's awesome. I love that. I've always wanted to boat. Do you ski or wakeboard or, or—" she started getting really excited "—I heard there's this crazy new trend of surfing behind a boat. I went to the ocean once with my parents. Oceanside, California. It was incredible, but I was a complete failure at surfing. So sad. I couldn't even boogie board without my dad basically throwing me onto the waves. Too wimpy of a swimmer."

He gave her a short laugh. "I could teach you to surf, behind a boat and in the ocean. I'm pretty good at both."

"What? Where did you do real surfing?"

"I was a Navy SEAL. We spent a lot of time close to the ocean. One of my men, Ryker, is an incredible surfer, so he taught all of us on days off."

"Oh, my goodness, I'm so jealous right now. Would you really teach me to surf behind a boat and on the ocean, or are you just being nice and placating me?"

He turned to face her. His dark eyes swept over her face and she could see conflict in them. He swallowed and nodded. "I said I would. My word is my bond."

With that, he turned and started walking again. Tess was in danger of swooning right on the edge of this creek. His word was his bond. Wow. That was incredible, not very common in this day, and did she dare even think it ... the sexiest thing she'd ever heard out of a man's mouth. She walked quietly for a few beats as the happy realization washed over her. They now had plans for after this week. She didn't dare hope that this stud of a man could be interested in her, but ... maybe?

"You're supposed to keep talking," he reminded her.

She laughed. How great was he that he liked to hear her talk? She'd think her handsome military stud wanted peace and quiet. "Okay," she said. "So what do your parents do for work?"

"My dad owns a fabrication shop. He worked hard to build it up and it's gone pretty well for him, but he works a lot of hours. My mom's a dental hygienist."

"No, stinking, way!" she screamed.

He spun. "What? Did you see something?"

She put a hand to her heart. "My mom's a dental hygienist. What are the odds?"

He gave her half a smile and shrugged.

"That is so cool. No wonder you have such great teeth. My dad's a dentist, so I got it both ways. I couldn't even have a lollipop as a kid."

"That's rough. My mom wasn't that strict."

"Lucky you. The neighbors had to sneak me candy. On Halloween, everybody respected my parents and had lame treats like pencils and dollar toys set aside for me when I came trick-or-treating, but some of them would give me candy when my parents weren't looking."

He gave her a fuller smile and started walking again. "So no sugar at all at your house?"

"My mom made cookies and cakes, occasionally we'd get donuts or ice cream, but candy and pop were on the absolute no list. I know, deprived childhood. I need a therapist or something." She laughed but stopped when she realized he wasn't laughing.

Silence ensued. What had she said wrong? Maybe he'd had a deprived childhood? Dang, what should she say now?

"So do you have any siblings?" he asked, thankfully breaking the silence.

"No. My parents created the perfect child and didn't want to risk messing up on a second one."

He did laugh then, and she felt much better.

"Truly, I always wanted a sister. Begged for one, actually, and I think I made my mom cry. I feel bad now, but as a young girl I was clueless. My mom was forty when they had me. They got married later in life, so I guess things just stop working when you're older. I know my mom wanted another baby too. What about you? Siblings? You said a sister, right?"

"Yes, I have a younger sister. She's amazing."

"Ah, I love that. The tough military man is all soft and squishy about his sister."

He chuckled and said, "If you met her, you'd like her. And she'd like you."

"Really? That means a lot, truly." She put a hand to her heart. He thought highly of his sister and thought she and Tess would like each other. How sweet was that? Unless it meant he thought of Tess as a little sister. She wrinkled her nose and stewed far too hard on that worry. "Tell me about her," she requested to hide her confusion.

"Kinsley. She's a lot like you—bubbly, fun, likes to talk. She also loves adventure."

Her hopes were waning. He thought of her as a little sister. It was better than thinking she was an annoying assignment, but any hopes of romance might be dashed. "Does she actually take adventures or just dream about them and watch them on television like me?"

He laughed. "She actually takes them. She moved to Colorado to be a river raft tour guide in the summer and a ski instructor in the winter."

"Wow. She is a tough one. Impressive. So tell me about ... other women in your life."

"What do you mean?" His voice was guarded now.

She bit at her lip and said bravely, "Do you have a wife, a girlfriend?"

"No wife or girlfriend," he said shortly. It was one of those stern, end-of-discussion kind of responses. Uh-oh. On one hand, she should be thrilled he wasn't attached. On the other, she was terrified that she'd stepped on a land mine. Had he recently been dumped? What kind of idiotic woman would dump the likes of

Britton Grady? She'd never met anyone that thick in the head. He was the catch of the century.

Wait, what had Axel said about his loss? Somebody had obviously died. Right? Isn't that what a loss would mean?

"Tess!" he cried out, interrupting her stewing. It was the most excitement she'd heard out of him.

"What?" Her gaze darted around, looking for wild pigs or a man in a loin cloth with a spear or a ... large Ziploc bag flapping from a tree. "Oh my heck," she screamed. "You found the treasure! And on the first day. I'm so stoked right now!"

He reached up and untied the bag from the tree branch. Tess stepped in closer so she could see what the treasure was. This was insane. Could they really have found it that easily? That quickly? She felt a pang of sadness that she wouldn't spend more time with this impressive man, but her charity and that half a million to help feed little ones and educate them and their parents had to take priority.

Even the unflappable Brit seemed excited. His hand trembled slightly and he hurriedly opened the Ziploc type bag and pulled out ... a bunch of gift wrap paper. They searched frantically through it, looking for a small jewel or something. Brit lifted a small note card and held it up.

"Your treasure is absolutely beautiful," he read aloud. He blinked and searched half-heartedly through the sack as if hoping for more.

Tess felt the letdown as well. "Your treasure is absolutely beautiful," she repeated. "Okay. It's a clue, so that's exciting." She didn't feel excited though. Of course a treasure would be beautiful. That was a defining characteristic of a treasure. Axel hadn't mentioned any clues, and this one didn't give them any direction on where to dig or which tree or mountain to climb.

She glanced around. "Do you think we should ... look around this spot? Maybe the treasure is close to the clue thing?"

"Sure." He put everything back in the bag and put it in his backpack. They searched all around the area. The sun dipped behind the trees as they looked and looked and found ... nothing. He checked his watch. "We were almost to the mile mark. Should we get there and then head back? We can move quicker going back."

"All right." It was so disappointing to think they'd found something and then nothing. Yet there was something in her that didn't mind spending more time with this tough, appealing man.

CHAPTER FOUR

Neither of them said much as they made it to the mile mark, stopped to fill their water bottles in the stream, took a long drink, and then hurried back along the creek. Tess kept her gaze on his strong back and he safely guided her. It was almost full-black as they reached their little camp.

They worked together to use the small propane stove and heat up one of the pre-made meals, a vegetable-beef stew that was actually pretty tasty. Brit asked some questions about Tess's little town and she happily told him about how quaint it was and how there were pine trees like the name and it wasn't as hot as most of Arizona because of the elevation.

As they finished eating, he pulled out the toothbrushes and toothpaste they'd found in the pack with the extra clothes and towels. "At least our moms will be happy we can brush our teeth."

She laughed and took one. "Thanks."

They brushed, spitting in the bush behind the tent and then rinsing the toothbrushes with their water bottles.

"Well, I guess we go to sleep now. Unless you want to play cards." Brit seemed as uncertain as she felt.

"Do you want to swim?" she asked.

From the flickering camp light on their small table, she saw his brows raise. "Swim?"

"I'm all sweaty and would love to swim so I can sleep without feeling so gross."

"And here you say you're not adventurous," he gently teased.

Tess laughed. "I'm trying."

"Okay," he agreed.

They walked along the creek. She'd taken off the GoPro when they got back to camp and she didn't put it back on. They had a lot of footage from today anyway and they'd get more tomorrow. They eased past the helipad to the pool under the waterfall. As they moved away from the light, it took a few seconds for Tess's eyes to adjust to the night. A half-moon provided a little light and stars twinkled above them. It was beautiful out here, especially as she gazed up at the towering waterfall cascading down the now-dark green flora.

She looked over the pool as they reached the edge and some of her bravery slipped away. "Do you think there's anything in there?"

"Nothing dangerous," he said. "Maybe some fish." He lifted his shirt over his head and draped it over a bush, leaning down to untie his shoelaces. There had been flip flops in the bottom of the clothing bucket, but they'd forgotten to grab them.

Even in the dark, she could see him far too well. She stared in awe at the muscles in his shoulders, arms and back as he unlaced then pulled off his shoes and socks. He straightened and caught her staring. "What?"

The muscles in his chest and abdomen were as glorious as every other part of him.

"Uh ... you're stinking beautiful, that's what." It flashed through her mind that the treasure was "beautiful." Not as beautiful as him.

He jolted and she couldn't see his eyes well enough to get a firm read on it, but she thought she'd embarrassed him.

"Sorry," she said. "You already know I talk far too much. Forget I said anything. You go swim."

"You're swimming too. You're the one that came up with the idea."

"Well I can't just strip my shirt off, can I?"

"Well, um ..." She'd obviously made him uncomfortable. "I won't look."

"Oh." That was almost as disappointing as thinking they'd found the treasure when they hadn't. He didn't even find her attractive. Otherwise he would probably find it impossible not to look. What did she expect? She didn't have some model-perfect shape; she was far too curvy and short. She was simply a naïve girl with no world experience who had talked far too much today. He was the perfect specimen, a military hero, and a super nice guy. Women probably chased him everywhere he went.

"There are plenty of extra clothes for both of us. If you want to swim in your t-shirt and shorts, you could change into dry clothes in the tent after."

It wasn't a bad plan. She took off her shoes and socks and started wading into the water. It was chilly, but she was hot and sticky so it felt wonderful.

"It's nice, eh?" Brit asked.

"Really nice."

He waited a short distance away. Tess waded toward him. Even though he'd said there was nothing dangerous in this water, she preferred being close to him. She was thigh-deep when the bottom changed from silty sand to uneven rocks. Tess stumbled and fell forward. She splashed face first into the water. She inhaled in surprise and it went down the wrong tube. She choked and gasped for air.

Arms surrounded her and lifted her out of the water. Brit held her close to his warm chest with one arm while he lifted her left arm up into the air. "You're okay, I've got you," he said.

Tess coughed and coughed, finally clearing her airway. The coughing calmed and she pulled in a few ragged breaths. Brit lowered her arm but held on to her as if she'd drown if he let go. His arms around her felt ... incredible, outstanding, better than the massage jets in her parents' hot tub. She was warm and tingly all over just being close to him.

He looked concerned, so she smiled to reassure him. "I told you I've never had adventures. Ten steps into a waterfall pool and I would've drowned in waist-deep water if you hadn't rescued me."

He chuckled and she joined him. His chuckle turned into full-blown laughter. She loved it, loved hearing him laugh, loved making him laugh, loved being close to him.

His laughter calmed and he looked her over with the most appealing smile. "Oh, Tess, I like you."

"You *do?*" She ignored her own stupid question and wasted no time wrapping her arms around that broad, beautiful, strong, firm back of his and tilting her head up, moistening her lips in what she hoped was an appealing way.

He stared down at her as if she was the most beautiful

woman he'd ever encountered. Her heart thumped out of control and she thanked her lucky stars, the good Lord above, and Axel Dexter for making this moment possible. Forget finding treasure. Brit was more important than any treasure she could imagine.

His head slowly lowered toward hers. His arms surrounded her lower back and pulled her flush against his glorious chest and she happily awaited the moment of impact. His lips would claim hers and her life would officially be perfect.

Brit's gaze traveled over her face and suddenly ... he froze. Like, absolutely froze. His body stiffened against hers. She'd already been experiencing the beauty of his incredible muscles before, but right now they were so rock hard and rigid they were almost ... scary.

"What is it?" She cowered against him. "Bears, wolves, feral pigs?"

Brit let out an unsteady laugh and released her from his arms. He stepped back and said quickly, "It's nothing."

With those lame words, he ducked under the water. He rose up and pushed the water back from his hair and wiped a hand over his face.

Tess was in awe at how glorious he looked, all tough and shiny with water droplets streaming down him, but she was confused and honestly ticked that he'd pulled away from her like that. What happened to her kiss of a lifetime? What had she done? Something she said?

"We'd better head back and get some rest," he said in a tight voice, like it hurt to speak. "Do you want to float or swim or are you ready?"

"Um, just one second." She followed his example and bent down low, letting the water cover her head, and swirled her fingers through her hair. Pushing back up, water ran down her face and dripped from her hair. She blinked the water from her eyes and caught him staring at her with a slightly open mouth. "What?" she questioned. "Is something hanging out? Did I do something?" She checked, but her t-shirt covered the essentials.

"No, nothing," he said shortly. "We should go." He reached out his arm, as if to take her arm and escort her, but then he quickly pulled his hand back and gestured for her to go first.

Tess pushed through the water in front of him, completely confused. One second, he seemed interested in her; the next, it was as if he didn't dare touch or look at her. They retrieved their shoes, slid them on, and walked quietly back to camp. Tess was bursting to say something, ask something, but she didn't know how to phrase it. He'd said he liked her, but maybe he hadn't meant it like she'd hoped he meant it. If he liked her in *that* way, he would've kissed her.

He waited outside the tent while she changed into dry clothes, a dri-fit tank top and spandex shorts that fit surprisingly well, as if someone knew her size. Finished changing, she ducked outside, hung her wet clothes to dry, and then pulled out the flip flops, which were also the right size. Those would be really nice after they explored all day in their tennis shoes. She finger-brushed her hair, wondering how frizzy the curls looked.

Part of her worried that climbing into the tent together would be awkward.

It was so much worse than she'd imagined.

Brit muttered something about how he'd sleep by the door. Tess slid out of her flip flops, stepped carefully over his spot, and laid on top of the thin pad and blanket. Even with her hair wet, she was still pretty warm. That was mostly due to the man stepping into the tent behind her. He heated her up, probably without even meaning to.

His shoulder brushed her arm as he settled next to her. She pulled in a quick breath and heard him do the same. For a long, drawn-out moment, the only sound was their ragged breathing. Static electricity arced between them and she was two seconds from combusting from the energy and anticipation zinging in the air. Did she dare roll toward him and just touch one part? Just his arm or shoulder. She wouldn't do anything crazy like touch his face or his chest.

She swallowed hard, dredged up all her courage, and lifted one hand. It was crazy how slow it moved and how it felt like it was no longer part of her body. She ached to touch him and maybe nudge their relationship closer, but she was terrified he'd reject her again.

As her hand brushed his shoulder, he jolted, tensed, and then rolled quickly away from her, facing the tent door. Her hand was in midair, trembling from the touch and abrupt rejection.

"Goodnight," he murmured.

Tess's hand slowly returned to her side. She couldn't bring herself to respond. Rejection was heavy in the tent. She fought the urge to sniffle and refused the desire to cry. She hardly knew Brit. The fact that he was in no way interested in her and was trying to make sure she knew that shouldn't feel like she'd lost the love of her life.

She pushed out a disgusted sigh at herself and rolled away to face the tent wall. It would be a very long week if she couldn't figure out how to hide how invested she already was in him.

CHAPTER FIVE

Brit hardly slept. He could feel and hear Tess; she was far too close to him. He didn't dare move and maybe brush against her or something. Who knew what he'd do then? His shoulder fell asleep—the thin mat was no match for the hard ground—but he didn't do anything to alleviate his discomfort.

He was disgusted with himself. Yes, Tess was incredibly appealing. Holding her close had been a heaven he couldn't remember experiencing since Kelley, maybe not even then if memory served correct, but that was no excuse for him to cuddle her in and almost kiss her. It was unfair to lead her on.

But was he leading her on? That was a terrifying question. He was interested in her, attracted to her, and could never remember being this impressed with anyone, especially this quickly.

He could not forget his promise to Kelley. He hadn't forgotten in almost twelve years. What was happening to him? Maybe his busy military life and limited dating opportunities had made it easier to keep his promise. Now that he was home permanently, he'd be around gorgeous, intriguing women more often. He'd have to be stronger, lock his heart better.

As he laid there throughout the uncomfortable night, sometimes drifting off but mostly just listening to Tess's sweet exhales and replaying how she'd felt pressed against him in the waterfall pool, he tried to remember Kelley. The picture in his mind of Kelley's face and dark eyes had faded over the years, but usually he could still envision her and remember the fun times they had together. Not right now. Right now, he saw aqua green eyes with those long, swoopy lashes and that happy sparkle. As he tried to picture Kelley's thinner face shape, he saw Tess's more rounded cheeks and those dimples. He loved those dimples, her innocence, the way she seemed unaware of her own appeal and beauty. Had he hurt her by pulling away and acting so abrupt? He groaned out loud.

"Brit?"

Ah, crap. She wasn't sleeping soundly as he'd hoped. He froze, held his breath, counted slowly in his mind to thirty.

"Brit?" Her voice pitched up. She wrapped her smooth arm around his chest and put her palm flat over his heart. Brit's body flared in response and his heart raced out of control. He pulled in a quick breath and was afraid he gasped like a little girl.

"Oh, Brit, you're breathing. I'm sorry if I woke you, but I had to check for a heartbeat. You stopped breathing for, like, a minute. That scared me."

Brit had no clue what to say or do. If he let himself roll onto his back, he was going to pull her close and kiss her. His weak brain envisioned doing just that while his body enjoyed her hand gently rubbing along his chest and her body pressed against his back.

"I'm fine," he gritted out, seconds away from losing all control, forgetting his integrity and the promise he made to Kelley, grabbing Tess, and kissing the rest of the night away. He even let himself rationalize for a brief second. He'd promised Kelley he wouldn't fall in love—he hadn't promised he wouldn't kiss another woman. But there was no way he could kiss the energetic, appealing Tess and not take another step down the road to losing his heart. He was much weaker than he'd ever imagined.

"Oh." Tess's voice sounded full of sadness and frustration. "I'm glad you're okay. Do you have sleep apnea or something?"

"No." Then he admitted something he shouldn't have. "I was holding my breath so you'd think I was asleep and go back to sleep yourself."

"Oh." She yanked her hand away and rolled onto her back. His body immediately ached for the loss of contact with her and yearned to have it back. It took more control and strength than running through the deserts of Afghanistan in full gear to escape the danger of grabbing her and hauling her close again. He couldn't imagine anything that sounded better than simply holding her.

No, he was lying to himself. Kissing her would be better.

"Well, if you want to fake sleep, you should try controlled breaths instead of holding your breath. Honestly, everybody knows that. Mr. Military Hero doesn't even know how to fake sleep." She let out a huffy little breath and it was all he could do not to laugh. She was exasperated and angry and he didn't blame her, but it was so cute. He'd never heard anyone cuss someone in such an appealing way.

"Thanks for the tip," he managed, faking slow, long breaths.

"Wow, you've really sold me this time."

Brit laughed. Instead of getting more upset with him, Tess laughed too. Their laughter filled the tent and even though he wouldn't let himself roll over and touch her, he could share a laugh with her. It was close to the feeling of touching her. His laughter hadn't come often since Kelley died. He'd laughed with his men—some of them were hilarious and could make anybody laugh—but he'd also held himself detached as their leader. The closest he'd come to a deep human connection like this was with his parents and sister, but he didn't see them near enough.

His laughter stopped abruptly. It wasn't fair to Tess to feel this deep connection to her when he could never progress in a relationship with her. He said, "Thanks. I think I can sleep now."

"Well, I hope so," she said to his back. "No more holding your breath. Next time, I'll give you mouth to mouth and shock the bejeebies right out of you. 'Night."

Brit's heart raced again and the tension from before filled the tent.

Mouth to mouth.

He let his mind wander around a kiss for far too long. He was breathing so hard he felt like he was running sprints. Round and round his mind went. He should just roll over, kiss her, and break this tension, get the need for her out of the way. No, that was wrong. He'd be a jerk to her and Kelley if he did that.

He tried to calm his own breathing and then noticed that her breathing had grown slow and steady. Disappointment and relief warred within him. She was either faking it or had actually fallen asleep. What would she do if he woke her up with a kiss?

Kelley, Kelley, Kelley. He repeated the name a hundred times, but it didn't help. He'd been semi-tempted by beautiful women a few times over the years, but he'd always prevailed. The other women had been nowhere close to Tess though. Tess was in a league of her own. How was he going to survive the next five days?

He closed his eyes tightly and prayed for help and strength, but he got nothing. Was Kelley up there watching over him, frustrated with his lack of commitment to her? He'd thought of her often as his guardian angel, but he didn't want her watching right now.

Brit blinked open his eyes. Dawn was approaching. Tess's soft exhales reassured him that at least one of them was sleeping. He'd been trained to perform at a high level without sleep or food, so he'd be fine, but she needed the rest.

He hoped he wouldn't wake her, but he couldn't take one more second in this tent. He slowly sat up and made the mistake of glancing at her. Even though it was still semi-dark, he could easily make out her curls falling across her neck, the pursing of her rosebud lips, the swell of her curves half-covered by her blanket. His hand lifted and slowly moved toward her face. He just wanted to touch one smooth cheek. That was all; a simple touch.

Centimeters from contact, his hand trembled with the need to touch her, cup that cheek in his palm, maybe caress her dimple. That was all he needed. A touch would get him through, then he'd be strong again.

His fingers rested on her cheek first and then he slowly, carefully slid them up to her cheekbone as his large palm easily cupped her jaw. He let out a breath of relief. This was heaven.

Her eyelids fluttered open. He should've jumped and run for safety. Instead, he met her gaze and felt the world settle around him.

"Morning," she whispered.

Brit couldn't find his voice to respond. All he could do was cup her cheek. She stared at him as if uncertain whether he would kiss her or run. He definitely needed to do the latter, and soon, but right now, even the President couldn't get him to move.

Slowly, her beautiful smile blossomed on her face. Her dimples appeared and his thumb moved to trace one. She pulled in a quick breath and her dimple disappeared. She sat up and he found himself rotating toward her, his hand sliding down her arm and then he reached her waist. As his palm cupped her hip, he found himself fascinated by the gentle curve of it and he lifted his other hand and framed her small waist in his palms.

The look in her eyes said she was every bit as enamored with him and his touch as he was with her. Her hands went to his shoulders and he pulled in a quick breath at the contact. Had anything ever felt so good, so right?

A rooster *cock-a-doodle-dooed* right next to the tent. Brit jumped and cursed. Tess laughed, showing once again how easygoing and fun she was, but Brit had already pulled his hands from her. Reality slapped him in the face harder than the rooster's annoying crow jarred his eardrums. He rocked away from Tess and unzipped the tent. Scurrying outside, he surveyed the rooster strutting around.

Tess climbed out and stood close to him, her bare arm brushing his and setting off a fire inside of him all over again. That was it. He had to find some way to keep his distance and his self-control. Many times throughout the past twelve years, he'd questioned if Kelley would really expect him to live his life all alone, to never fall in love. But he'd made the promise and he knew she would've kept her end if he had died. She was the instigator of the "solemn vow on the Holy Bible," after all.

"How do you think that crazy rooster got clear out here?" Tess asked, staring up at him. Her eyes were incredible.

"I don't know." He forced a laugh and stepped away from her. Sliding into his flip flops, he added, "I saw egg skillets in the food box. That okay for breakfast?"

Not waiting for an answer, he rushed for their supplies. The sooner they ate and got on their way, the better. They'd found a clue yesterday. Heaven willing, they'd find the treasure today and he could put this assignment behind him.

An assignment.

He had to find a way to look at this beautiful woman as an assignment or he'd be sunk.

CHAPTER SIX

Tess followed Brit through the thick jungle. The prospect of finding anything in this almost impenetrable wall of trees and undergrowth was growing dimmer by the minute. It was Tuesday evening, almost through their second day, and they'd found nothing. Not for lack of trying. They'd pushed themselves hard and Tess's body felt it. She'd lost track of how many miles they'd traversed. Brit had plotted out the area they needed to cover last night and figured out how they could miss very little. They walked straight for a short while, then started weaving toward their mile marker, doing the same thing on the way back so as not to miss anything. He used his watch and his instincts to make sure they covered all the ground. She didn't know how they could possibly get through all the area before Saturday evening. Hopefully they would find something before then.

A few helicopters flew overhead and they even talked to one group of tourists on their lunch break, but that was the most exciting thing that had happened today. Tess's feet hurt from walking and stumbling over branches and rocks, her legs hurt from overuse, her back hurt from sleeping on that thin mat, her head and neck hurt from staring at her feet, but her heart hurt worse than anything.

After Brit had given her one of the most tender touches and glances she had ever felt, he'd pulled away and had been distant the rest of this miserable day. He wasn't rude—quite the opposite. He held branches out of the way for her and periodically checked on her to make sure she was all right, but he was very, very careful not to touch her or encourage any daydreams on his end. She would've thought she repulsed him if she didn't have the memory of waking up to him cupping her cheek and running his thumb over her dimple in the sweetest gesture known to man. Then his hands wrapping around her waist had filled her with desire and anticipation, until he'd broken away.

She forced herself to look up and around for treasure rather than studying her feet as they traipsed through the path of least resistance. At first, she had been concerned they'd miss spots where the treasure might be, but the more tired she got, the less she cared. Brit hadn't even said anything about her not talking today.

"That's the mile," he said, stopping and stretching, touching branches above him with his long arms. He swung off his backpack, took out his water bottle, and took a long swallow. She should've followed suit but she simply stared at him, the way the muscles in his arms flexed as he held the water bottle, a trickle of water spilling down his lip. She wanted to move in close and taste that moisture.

Looking away, she cursed herself. He wasn't interested in her;

or if he was, he was fighting it very well. She needed to refrain from throwing herself at him.

"You doing all right?" he asked quietly.

"It's been a right bummer of a day," she admitted.

He nodded. "I know, not finding even a clue."

"I'm not talking about the treasure." Of course she wanted that treasure for her charity, desperately, but this trip was becoming about a lot more than money for her.

He froze with his water bottle halfway to his mouth. Their gazes caught and held. Maybe she should feel bad for calling him out, but he needed to know how she felt. She stared into his deep brown eyes, feeling lost and never wanting to be found, except by him.

He broke from her gaze and said, "We'd better head back. The sun will be gone soon."

Tess pushed out a breath of frustration, took a quick drink from her own water bottle, and followed him. Tess was tired of the quiet and tired of not knowing how to read him, but she was also tired of acting like a wilting flower. She'd promised she wouldn't complain, and she hadn't, but she'd also been quiet and morose all day, which definitely wasn't like her.

All she could control was herself and her own attitude. Her parents and her church leaders had taught her that, and she knew it was true. She forced a smile, even though he wasn't looking back to see it, and she immediately felt better.

As they plodded back to camp, she started talking, asking him about each of the men he'd served with. He seemed relieved and told her stories about Professor, Cowboy, Preacher, and the surfer boy, Ryker. She kept asking him questions to keep him talking and before she knew it, they were approaching camp.

"Any requests for dinner?" he asked as they dropped their backpacks and she happily took the GoPro off.

"Let's find that rooster, kill it, pluck it, and roast it," she said, only partially teasing. Roasted chicken sounded really good right now.

He chuckled and she joined in. "I think that rooster would be tougher than your tennis shoe."

"Ah, don't ruin my fantasies of some *fried* chicken." She tried to infuse a Southern accent.

He laughed again and started rifling through their supplies. He held up a couple of the premade meals. "Chicken teriyaki and veggies or beef pasta marinara?"

"Better go with the chicken, since I'm craving it and all."

"Sounds good."

He seemed much more relaxed than he had all day. Talking on the way back from their last mile must've helped him realize she wasn't going to pin him down in the tent and kiss him, no matter how badly she wanted to. Everything did feel better with a smile on her face. They hadn't found any clues or treasure, but they'd covered a lot of ground. They were arcing in a circle and tomorrow they would reach their side of the waterfall. Traversing that incline would be rough.

"I've got to use the restroom," she admitted.

"Be careful."

She liked that he cared, but it was probably only because he was her protection detail. "Thankfully, no snakes here so I'm sure I'll be fine." She took a roll of toilet paper and a partially-filled garbage bag. Walking down the stream a little ways, she went off into the thick foliage until she found a dead tree to lean over. She heard snorting and snuffling. Her eyes widened. Several baby pigs waddled into view, snuffling along the side of the creek.

"Oh my goodness, those are adorable!" she exclaimed. Hurrying to stand up and stash her used toilet paper in the bag, she pulled her shorts into place and all but ran toward the baby pigs. "How cute are you?" she asked. Her neighbor had pigs. When they got big, they were some of the smelliest, most disgusting animals on the planet, but as babies they were so stinking cute. Her neighbor had let her help feed the babies since she was a small child.

One of the piglets snuffled right up to her.

"Hello, cutie," she said, bending down to pet the teeny animal.

"Tess!" a sharp yell sounded from behind her.

Turning, she was surprised to see Brit running at her.

"Brit! Baby pigs. First a rooster and now pigs." She clapped her hands together in delight.

"Tess, run!"

Something slammed into her from behind. Tess screamed as she hit the rocks and undergrowth face first. Whatever had tackled her smelled like poopy garbage and was covered in bristly hair. The animal smashed her into the ground, digging at her back with its hard ... something. Was it the piglets' mother? The momma pigs at home had never cared that she played with their babies, but maybe pigs in the wild acted differently. She had no clue, but she was going to suffocate or crack a rib from the pressure.

She heard a loud, deep yell and then the pig was flipped off of her. Tess groaned and slowly rose to a seated position, watching as Brit wrestled the squealing, squirming pig to the ground, his arms wrapped tightly around her neck as the large animal snorted and tried to knock into him with her hooves and her head.

"Run, Tess!" he yelled. "Go to the other side of the stream so you aren't between her and the babies."

Tess pushed to her feet, shakily backing away. She wanted to help Brit somehow. The pig was trying to push from his iron grip and bite at him.

"Go!" Brit hollered.

She stumbled into the stream and sloshed through, checking over her shoulder to see if Brit was okay. The water was only up to her knees. She tried to move quickly, but she hit a rock and stumbled once. She could hear the pig squealing and Brit grunting as he restrained her.

As soon as she reached the other side, she turned. The piglets had hurried back to their mother, squeaking at her distress.

Tess wrung her hands together and prayed that Brit would be okay. He shoved the pig toward her piglets and then leapt away from them. The pig turned threateningly to him. Brit backed away and then hurried through the water and to Tess's side.

The pig snorted at him, then snuffled around her piglets as if checking if they were okay. Tess and Brit watched them. Together they eased toward the waterfall, waiting for the mother to come after them again. The piglets wandered back down the bank, thankfully away from their camp and the waterfall. The mama gave one last snort and followed them.

Tess watched them go and then turned to Brit. "Are you okay?"

He gave her a devil-may-care grin. "Just a little pig wrestle. No big deal."

Tess laughed in disbelief. She grabbed his arms and checked

him over. He was a little scratched up, but he did seem fine. "Oh, Brit." She let out a little whimper. "You saved me." Then she flung her arms around his neck, pulled herself up close to his face, and kissed him.

Brit stiffened and she feared he'd push her away. His lips were firm and felt amazing against hers, but he definitely wasn't responding. She started to pull back, but at that instant, he wrapped his arms around her, yanked her against his chest, and kissed her back. It was a kiss she'd never fathomed actually existed. She'd been kissed before, but the passion, strength, commitment, and connection between them was unparalleled and may never be replicated in this lifetime, at least not for her.

As fast as this incredible kiss began, it was abruptly severed. Brit wrenched himself from her, stepped a respectable distance away, and pushed a hand through his hair. "Oh, Tess, I apologize. The adrenaline and the relief that you're okay and then you kissed me and I ... I am so sorry, Tess." He looked to where the pigs had disappeared. "Please forgive my rash behavior."

Tess's mouth dropped open. For half a second, she could only stare at him. She lost her tongue, but found it quickly. "Whoa, whoa, whoa. Back up the stinking school bus. You kissed me like that, like it's the epic end of Star Wars and you're Kylo Ren and I'm Rey and you're going to fizzle into nothingness after this kiss ends ..." She paused for breath. "And thank heavens to Star Wars, by the way, for *finally* getting a kiss right, but that isn't the subject here at all." She had to focus, but his kiss had scattered every brain cell. He still wasn't looking at her and she really wanted him to look at her. "So you were just all in the heat of the moment and I kissed you, but then you kissed me back—dang, man, you kissed me back, you know you did. And you kissed me thoroughly. Now you're going to apologize and pretend the kiss didn't mean anything to you?" She made herself stop, giving him a chance to redeem himself.

He slowly turned his head and met her gaze. His dark eyes were full of abject misery. That look wrenched her heart. They stared at each other and there was no need for him to apologize any further. She'd seen into his heart in that moment. She had no idea why, but she knew ... He didn't want to hurt her, and for some reason, he was being torn in two.

She blinked at him and then gave him an out. "Do you need some time to work this crap out in your mind?"

He stared at her as if she were an apparition and admitted, "Yes, please."

She drew in a steadying breath. Something was horribly wrong inside Brit. She never would've guessed the fabulous and tough military man was a mess inside. PTSD? Lost his team? Killed innocents and it had rent his soul in two? Maybe something to do with the loss that Axel had mentioned? Could that mean a wife or girlfriend? Brit had said he didn't have a wife or girlfriend, but that could mean currently. She had no idea, but the thought of dragging his secrets out didn't sit right.

She said a prayer for Brit and for her to know how to help him and then changed the subject. "Do you want to swim? I feel disgusting and all I did was walk all day, then get knocked to the ground by a pig. You wrestled with that disgusting pig. Can you believe how much it stunk? I have neighbors with pigs and they stink, believe me they do, but they don't stink that much. So gross."

She wondered if the cameras that covered their camping spot had caught the pig fight or the kiss. She'd tried to angle them in all directions. Was that why Brit was struggling? He didn't like the cameras being privy to his personal life? No, that miserable look in his eyes had been much deeper than stage fright.

She splashed back into the river and he walked by her side. "Did you spend much time with the neighbors' pigs?" he asked as if trying to keep up his end of the conversation.

They both took off their wet tennis shoes and slid into flip flops as she talked. She told him about the pigs and how she'd loved the babies, which was why she hadn't thought twice about approaching these babies. On and on she blabbed. He contributed to the conversation, but remained distant. When he pulled his shirt over his head to swim, she tried not to stare. She had to figure out some way to steel her heart to this man. He was the most appealing and incredible man she'd ever been around, but he obviously couldn't or wouldn't reciprocate those feelings, so she needed to somehow push them away. That stunk. She'd had the best kiss of her life, and highly doubted it would ever happen again.

CHAPTER SEVEN

Brit tried not to stare with an open mouth as Tess floated not far from him. She was beautiful for sure, but her appeal to him was far more than her pretty little motor-mouth, aqua-colored eyes, and curvy shape. He loved being around her and that kiss had rocked him all the way to his core. He had to be completely honest with himself; even his memories of kissing Kelley were not comparable to the kiss he'd just shared with Tess. Yes, there had been a lot of adrenaline from watching Tess be flattened by a feral momma pig and fighting the pig himself, and then the relief of knowing she was okay, but he didn't believe that had anything to do with how that kiss had affected him.

Then she'd been so cute, telling him off while expostulating about Star Wars kisses. He'd thought she would demand to know what he was feeling and discuss every angle of those feelings, but again she'd shocked him by giving him an out and then offering to come swim.

He swam away from her and up close to the waterfall. Unfortunately, it wasn't free-falling enough to swim under, since Brit could've really used the pounding on his head. Tess was amazing. He didn't know anyone else who would've let him off the hook like that and then just adorably talked about pigs as if nothing had happened. When their eyes had met after the kiss, she'd seemed to see into his soul and then decide to take pity on his plight instead of cursing him for being a weak man.

He had never been so confused in his life. From the moment he'd made the promise to Kelley, he'd never doubted he would keep it. You didn't go back on swearing on the Bible. He'd regretted the vow over the years and hated the depressing feeling of knowing he'd never have a beautiful wife and family of his own, but he thought he'd dealt with it okay.

Right now, he wanted to beg the good Lord to send down Kelley's angel. If she descended from heaven and told him it was okay that he fell for Tess—knowing his teenage love wanted him to be happy and find love—he could move on without guilt.

He glanced back at Tess. She was treading water and gave him her happy, bright, beautiful smile.

Finding love with Tess sounded like the dream of a lifetime, but he'd never seen an angel and didn't know anyone who had. His hopes of Kelley freeing him from his vow took a deep plunge into the water.

He passed a hand over his face and swam back to Tess. "Clean enough for dinner?"

She laughed. "I don't think I'll be clean enough until we get back to showers, shampoo, and my coconut colada body wash, but this will suffice for now."

Coconut colada body wash? That sounded like a scent he'd

love to smell on her soft neck. He splashed water on his face and managed, "I'm with you."

They swam to where they could touch and then waded out of the pool. "You're with me?" she teased. "Coconut colada body wash for my tough military man?"

He smiled, wishing she wouldn't say "my." She had no clue how much he wanted to be hers. After two days of knowing her. He was losing it. Maybe depriving himself of growing close to a beautiful woman was making him crave it insanely now that he was here with Tess. He was like an alcoholic who'd been dry for years, pinned down, having shots of whiskey drizzled down his throat. "No coconut colada."

"What is your signature scent?" she asked as she dried her hair with one of the towels. He tried not to gape at her beautiful shape in the wet tank top and shorts.

"Duke Cannon sandalwood-musk cologne. My sister sent it to me when I was in Guam. It's a cool company that donates to military and vets and I really like the smell."

"Nice. I'll have to look them up. Any products for girls?"

"No, ma'am."

"Ah, I see how you military men are." She winked to show she took no offense. "I would love to smell that on you though ... Duke Cannon. Sandalwood and musk sounds incredible."

His heart picked up its beat and he could only stare at her. Someday, would she be able to smell his Duke Cannon and he could smell her coconut colada? He could too easily imagine bending down low to smell her neck, kissing it softly then working his way back up to her lips. He blinked to try to push away the vision. He didn't know if they could ever get to that day.

"It's crazy. It's only been two days and already it's hard to be stinky and ugly." She laughed easily.

"I don't think you're stinky or ugly," he said before he could stop himself.

She smiled sweetly and said, "Nothing could make you ugly in my eyes."

He felt like she'd smacked him upside the head with an assault rifle. He tried to joke, "But I stink right now? Is that what you're trying to say?"

She grinned. "Maybe you should get back in the waterfall pool."

He laughed, and then they worked together to prepare dinner. Brit was surprised how at ease he felt around her, but the slightest look could have him right back in that kiss, wishing he could do it all over again. He was careful not to touch her. Who knew what he'd do if he felt her soft skin under his fingertips again, or worse ... her body pressed close to his?

He needed to focus on Kelley, but it was almost impossible with Tess's sweet presence, easy nature, and happiness swirling around him. He felt infused with joy and happy future possibilities. That wasn't his reality, but in this tropical paradise with this perfect woman, he was far, far from reality.

Darkness surrounded them as they cleaned up their dinner. After brushing their teeth, he unzipped the tent and held the flap for her. He was glad to be done with cameras for the day. Tess always wore the GoPro when they were out looking for treasure, and the cameras around camp captured everything when she didn't have it on. He'd think he could relax without a camera recording everything he said and did, but there wouldn't be any relaxation tonight. The surge of tension surrounded him as soon as they entered the tent. He needed to push this desire for her away and sleep tonight. She lay down on top of her blanket and pad. He could make out her shape in the darkness. Zipping the tent shut, he tried to ease down without brushing against her.

"Would you care if we prayed together?" she asked into the darkness.

Prayed together? Brit pushed that around in his mind and felt the rightness of it settle deep within him. "I would love that," he admitted.

They both knelt on their pads and she extended her hands. He wrapped his around hers. Instead of pulsating desire, he felt a purity to their touch. The past two days, he'd muttered brief prayers and they'd prayed over the food, but he'd felt far from heaven. He hadn't had his scriptures or meetings with a pastor or a preacher. He'd never been picky about who he met with, as long as that person had the spirit with them, but he felt closest to his childhood pastor, Pastor Butler.

"Do you want me to say it?" she asked quietly into the silence.

"Sure. Thanks."

"Yep." She squeezed his hands and started a long, drawn-out prayer. He smiled to himself as she prayed, knowing he shouldn't have expected anything less from this woman who had chatter down to an art. Her prayer was meaningful and heartfelt as she blessed everyone from the President to the children in need to those children's parents being able to take good care of them to the veterans, military, police, firefighters, and healthcare workers. She went on and on, thanking the Lord for Brit's strength and protection of her and asking for help in finding the treasure so she could help the children.

As she finally said amen and he echoed it, sweet silence fell in the tent. She released his hands and laid down. "Thanks for being here, Brit," she said.

He laid down as well. "Thanks for being so great, Tess."

Her light laughter reached out to him. "It's a talent I have."

"Along with talking."

"Yes, sir. My dad says I can talk the hind legs off a mule."

"I like it," he admitted before he could catch himself.

"Thanks."

Neither of them said anything more but he didn't mind the silence. Brit listened to her breathing and the sound of the waterfall not far away. This day had taken him from boredom and frustration at not finding anything that would help Tess's cause to the best kiss of his life, and all the confusion and guilt that brought, to Tess showing him once again how great she was.

Through the past twelve years, he'd sometimes wished he hadn't made that promise to Kelley. He didn't want to spend his life without love, but never had he had such a huge reason to regret that promise. If only there was another solution besides breaking his word.

Breaking his word was something he knew he'd never do.

CHAPTER EIGHT

Tess slept better Tuesday night than she had Monday. After praying together, she'd felt a peace and a rightness to where she was and who she was with. She didn't know if Brit regretted their kiss or just had some reason he couldn't act on the feelings she thought he was developing for her, but she felt strangely okay about it all. That wasn't typical of her. Usually, she wanted to talk until she had a solution, but she felt heaven's calming influence on her.

She opened her eyes Wednesday morning and he was gone. Standing and stretching, she zipped open the tent and found him leaning over their supplies. Dang if he wasn't the finest-looking man she'd ever seen. He straightened and smiled at her, holding up a couple packages. "Strawberry granola?"

"I thought you'd never ask."

He kept his smile, but his eyes grew warm and deep. She lost herself in their depths for a second, but a helicopter slicing through the air pulled his gaze from her. "They're earlier today."

"Or are we later?" she asked. It was cloudy; they'd most likely get rain before the day was out. She hoped that wouldn't hinder their progress. They'd gone over a lot of area yesterday, even if they'd found nothing.

He checked his watch. "You're right. We were on the road by seven yesterday. It's already seven-thirty."

"On the road." She laughed dryly.

They ate quickly, brushed their teeth, filled their water bottles, and started on their trek. The nice thing about their strategy—walking a mile out and then weaving back—was they could refill supplies and water each time if needed.

As they walked, they searched high and low and he asked questions about her charity. She was happy to share all the different ways they'd been able to help children and parents in the Flagstaff area and the vision she had of expanding to other areas in Arizona and possibly into some third-world countries. Her focus was on basic needs first but then on teaching children, teenagers, and their parents to help themselves by growing gardens, increasing education and skills for their futures, but also teaching them about making smart choices with the money the parents earned or were given by the government. Many parents she worked with had never learned about frugality and smart choices.

Brit listened as she talked and asked questions. They walked and walked. A light drizzle started as they worked their way closer to the waterfall. The incline and decline of the terrain grew rougher.

Tess glanced down at one point and saw a shiny bag attached to some undergrowth. "Brit!"

Brit halted and spun around, hands up as if ready to fight to protect her. "What?"

"Another clue," she said, detaching the bag, praying it wasn't a clue but the treasure itself. Talking about her charity and the children for the past couple hours had reaffirmed why she was here and what she needed to accomplish. So many children were suffering. Her programs had helped many, not just with immediate needs but with seeing a brighter future through their own knowledge and work.

She opened the bag with trembling fingers, searching through the shiny gift-wrap paper, and pulled out another clue on cardstock. It was a disappointment to be sure and she could see it in Brit's eyes.

Your treasure is important.

Pushing out a breath of frustration, she said, "Well, that was earth-shattering."

Brit nodded, giving her a reassuring smile. "At least we found another clue."

"Yeah, true." They searched the area high and low but found nothing else. *Your treasure is important.* Did that give them any insight?

Finally, they gave up on the treasure being close by and she took a long drink from her water bottle. "I'm not sure if these clues are meant to be encouraging or frustrating." She winked. "Just kidding. I'm staying in good spirits. It'll all work out awesome."

Brit stared at her. "You are a master at staying in good spirits. I wish we could've had you with us on some missions just to keep everybody happy."

"Aw, thank you, my tough military hero." She grinned. "But I would've talked all of your ears off and probably drove Denzel and Tanner crazy." She referred to the educated professor and the one who'd been ditched by his girlfriend. If she was honest, she might've driven more of the men crazy than that.

He chuckled. "Only because they're ornery dudes. I like your chatter."

"Thanks." He did seem to like it and encouraged her talking. It made her like him even more. Did she dare think again that they could be a great fit? She probably shouldn't indulge in those thoughts with the way he'd shut her down after their kiss.

He turned and they started exploring again. Finding a clue actually did help reenergize her and get her excited about finding the treasure for her kiddos. It was better than yesterday when they'd found nothing. But yesterday she'd gotten the kiss of a lifetime. She doubted that was happening today. Brit had been great, but very careful not to touch her or get too close.

The rain continued after lunch and soon they were slogging through mud. Brit asked if she'd prefer to take a break for the day or explore a flatter area but she insisted they keep going with the pattern he'd set up so they didn't miss anything.

They navigated the section as close to the waterfall as they dared and then went the mile beyond along the river but above the waterfall this time. Walking by the river was easier, but the mud made them slip and slide and the rain was getting so thick it was hard to see. They hadn't seen any helicopter tours since lunch; probably called off because of low visibility.

They reached the mile mark and the rain had gotten steadily stronger. Brit said, "Are you okay if we navigate across the river and head back looking on that side? I don't know how tricky it will be to get down that side of the falls. I wouldn't have come up here again if I'd known the rain would get worse. My satellite phone said it was supposed to taper off after noon."

"We've got this," she said, forcing a smile. They were only up here because she was so insistent on keeping their search pattern. Hopefully, Brit wouldn't get hurt.

Even with a rain poncho on, she was wet and miserable. Lying side by side in their dry tent sounded wonderful about now. Thoughts of a delicious, home-cooked meal with her famous French bread and her mom's cookies, a shower with good-smelling shampoo and body wash, and dry clothes weren't reality, so she didn't let herself dwell there too long.

"Thanks for being so great," Brit said. He took her hand and she felt the rightness of his touch settle over her. Who needed dry clothes and delicious food when Britton Grady was walking by their side?

They navigated the river side by side. It wasn't bad, no worse than the muddy terrain they'd trekked through for the past hour. Wading through with her hand clasped in Brit's made it infinitely better. Sadly, he released her when they were safely on the other bank.

"This is a fun adventure," she said, focusing on staying upbeat.

"Thank you for staying so positive," Brit said. His tone was quiet but meaningful. A shiver of happiness slid through her.

Tess grinned, but the rain responded to her positivity by turning into a torrential downpour. They both chuckled at the irony and plunged forward, hoping to get back to camp and out of this wetness soon. She started to worry if their tent would be dry. Everything on this expedition was high quality, but it could be flooded from underneath. What if all their supplies were swept away and washed down the river? She shivered as they picked their way along the other side of the river above the waterfall. They reached the waterfall's edge and it was a crazy cool view from above with the increase in water flow from the rain. She hoped the GoPro could pick it up with all the misty moisture in the air.

"Do you think all our stuff will get washed away?" she asked.

"No," Brit reassured her. "The boxes were pretty heavy and we weren't on a slope or anything. I made sure the tent would stay dry when we placed it. You ready to make our way down?"

"Lead the way, oh military stud of mine," she said.

He gave her that smile that made her heart race, but she could read a sadness in his eyes. He could never be "hers," and he obviously didn't know how to tell her that. She should tell him that she got it, no matter how sad it made her they weren't a match. It wasn't an easy conversation to have.

They moved away from the waterfall. The descent would be easier away from the water. It was hard to see much at this point. Brit picked his way down the steep part, instructing her on where to grab and cautioning her to go slow. For the most part, there were lots of hanging branches or roots to hold on to when it got steep.

She was easing herself down a particularly steep part, clinging to a branch and actually feeling quite tough and adventurous, when she heard a sharp crack. The branch gave way. Her feet slid out from under her and she plunged down the incline. Catching her foot on an exposed root, she flung forward, felt her ankle twist weird, and cried out in pain. She was certain she'd go headfirst to her death, but Brit caught her arm and stopped her descent.

Tess was upside down, breathing hard. Was she still in one piece? She did a quick inventory. Her ankle throbbed, but everything else felt okay.

Brit cautiously wrapped his arms around her waist and started to lower her toward him.

"My ankle," she cried out. She tried to pull herself up to loosen it.

"Wait," Brit cautioned. "Hold on to this root. I'll climb up and untangle you."

"Okay." She clung to the root he showed her and hoped it wouldn't rip out or break like the last one. Blood filled her head, making it pound in response.

Brit quickly scaled back up and lifted her ankle free, holding on to her legs and slowly lowering her to a wide ledge. Finally, she was right side up, but as she put weight on her ankle, she cried out again.

"Broken?" Brit asked.

"I don't think so. Just a bad sprain." But a bad sprain could put her out of the running. Oh my, how was she going to get the treasure now? The more important question of the moment was how they were going to get down this treacherous slope and back to camp.

Brit hovered close by as she hung on to the root. "I'm sorry, Tess. We shouldn't have gone back down this steep part with the rain."

"I'm the one who insisted, remember?"

He nodded but said quietly, "But I have more experience in the field."

Her ankle hurt and she didn't know that she'd ever been more miserable, but she lifted her chin and said, "There's nothing to do but go forward now. Don't make me drag you back to camp."

He gave her a half smile and said, "You're incredible, do you know that?"

"Thanks." She didn't want to break his gaze, but she forced

herself to lower her weight down the slope and look for the next handhold.

Brit scrambled next to her, helping her find handholds and lifting her at times. His dexterity and strength was incredible. It took forever, but finally they were on level ground again, not too far from the waterfall pool and their camp, but on the wrong side of the river.

Brit swept her off her feet and cradled her against his chest. She lost the ability to breathe as she stared into his face. Water dripped down his cheeks and off his nose. He was the most beautiful man she'd ever seen.

Wrapping her arms around his neck, she pulled herself in tight to his chest as he carried her slowly through the jungle and to the river. Time went far too fast as he waded through the river with her in his arms and then they were back at camp. Neither of them said anything, but the power surging between them was off the charts. Would he kiss her again? He seemed to be battling with his self-control and she didn't want to push him, no matter how badly she wanted his kiss.

They reached camp and he held her tight for a second, staring down at her. "How's the ankle?"

Better than my heart, she wanted to say. "Not great," she admitted. "Hopefully I can walk it off."

He lifted his eyebrows as if he doubted that. "Let's get you into dry clothes and in the tent."

He let her feet slide to the ground and disappointment filled her. No kiss. She hoped for later but doubted he'd let his self-control slip again.

With his arm around her waist, though, she couldn't feel too much disappointment. She took off the GoPro. The cameras in camp would pick up their movements and words now. She found a dry t-shirt and shorts and he helped her into the tent to change, pushing their beds out of the way so she didn't drip on them. Thankfully it was still dry in there. It was hard to change while standing on one foot and trying to keep her wet stuff from getting everything else wet, but she managed.

"You ready?" Brit called from the other side of the tent.

"Yes, sir," she called back.

He unzipped the tent then knelt partway in. She set her wet clothes outside; they'd have to rinse them and hang them up when the rain stopped. Propping the tent flap so the rain would run down his back instead of inside the tent, he held up some medical tape. "Okay, sit down and I'll get this wrapped. Then I'll find you some food."

"You're going to get soaked like that," she scolded him.

"I'm already soaked." He gave her a charming smile. "I'd rather keep the tent dry so when I finally get in there with you, there's hope of getting some sleep tonight."

She cocked her head and studied him. "Have you not slept the other nights?"

He only lifted his eyebrows in response. A flush warmed her. Was she the reason he wasn't sleeping? She sat on the pile of bedding and lifted her ankle. He propped it on his muscular thigh as he knelt there. Her legs were muddy. He lifted one of their wet towels that he must've retrieved from a nearby bush and rubbed at the mud on her legs.

He glanced up at her as he worked. A thrill ran through her. With one look, he could have her begging for him to kiss her again. She shouldn't have given him an out last night after they kissed, but his look of anguish was still in her mind's eye. She couldn't cause him pain, and demanding to know why they couldn't kiss every other minute seemed as if it would do just that.

Tess felt like royalty as he cared for her, first cleaning her legs, drying them tenderly, and then wrapping her ankle.

When he finished, his warm palms lingered on her leg. "Better?" he asked, staring deeply into her eyes.

"Yes," she managed. She was milliseconds from grabbing him and dragging him into the tent with her when he gently put her leg down.

"I'll be right back with food," he said, scooping up her wet clothes, the wet towel, and the athletic tape.

She waited impatiently, not so much for the food but for his company. She didn't want to push him to kiss her or talk things through with her, but she wanted to be with him, every minute, every day. Would this newness and excitement ever wear off? She hoped not. She had to keep reminding herself that finding the treasure should be her focus. After this week, she probably wouldn't see him again.

At the moment, not even a sprained ankle, a ton of rain, and the prospect of a cold dinner could keep her down. She was with Brit. She wanted to savor that.

The flap opened again and Brit handed her a bag full of stuff. "This was all I could find that didn't need to be warmed up." He pulled back out and was back in a second with a roll of dry clothes for himself.

Tess scooted to the side with the bag of food and water bottles. Brit zipped the flap up, dripping like crazy.

"I need to change quick and get this wet stuff out of here," he said. "Can you ...?"

"Oh my, yes!" She squeezed her eyes shut and turned her head. Listening to him peel his clothes off made her heart race.

"Please, please keep my thoughts pure," she muttered in a prayer, and then felt her face flush as she heard him chuckle softly.

"Okay, I'm done," he said.

The tent zipper went up again. He must've shoved the wet clothes back out. Tess peeled her eyes open. His shirt and shorts clung to his lovely muscles. He sat down on the sleeping pad next to her. Water dripped from his face and hair.

Tess scooted close to him and swiped the water from his brow with the pads of her fingers. He stared at her, his mouth slightly open. The way he looked at her said she might get the second-best kiss of her life, but he only blinked and pulled slightly away. "Anything good in the food bags? I'm starving."

She laughed uneasily and sifted through the food. They ate a simple meal of protein bars, jerky, almonds, and dried fruit, washing it down with water from their water bottles and listening to the rain pounding the tent roof. He'd also found ibuprofen, so she downed four of those to help with the swelling. Luckily, her ankle only hurt when she put pressure on it.

"Hope this rain doesn't last," Brit said as he stacked the garbage and food next to the tent door and tried to rearrange their bedding while maneuvering around her. Every time he accidentally touched her, her stomach swirled with heat and her heart raced quicker.

"Me too. I really hope I can walk tomorrow."

He acknowledged that with a tilt of his chin. "Lay down and I'll prop up your ankle. That will help, but not as much as ice would."

"Okay, thanks."

She slid down on top of the blanket and pad. It felt good to stretch, and she let out a soft groan.

"You okay?" Brit asked.

"Um-hmm. It feels good to stretch out."

He gently propped up her ankle on his rolled blanket and then laid down on his pad, far too close for her susceptible frame of mind. Her heart raced and she felt like his nearness was getting harder to navigate, not easier. He made her want to fling herself into his arms, and that kiss was never far from her mind.

"That does feel good," he murmured. He tilted his head to the side. In the darkened tent, she could see the outline of his handsome face. "How are you doing, Tess?"

"I'm great." With him here, how could she be any different? "I mean, I would've preferred to brush my teeth after dinner and swim in the waterfall, but how can I complain when I've got a dry place to sleep and a full belly?"

He didn't say anything for a second and she wondered what was wrong. When his voice came, it was gravelly and low. "For someone who claims they've never done real adventure, you are sure handling this well."

"Ah, thank you."

"No, seriously. I've heard more complaining out of highly-trained Navy SEALs than I've heard out of you."

She put a hand to her heart. "That means a lot, but I'm sure your 'highly-trained Navy SEALs' wouldn't have fallen and twisted their ankles."

"Everybody has injuries, Tess. You haven't even complained about yours."

"It truly doesn't hurt that bad, thanks to your superior wrapping job."

He chuckled. "At the risk of gushing over you, thank you for having such a positive attitude. You remind me more of my sister every day."

She appreciated his compliment but wondered once again if he thought of her as a sister. It explained why he acted so weird when they got close. "Thanks," was all she said.

"Did your parents raise you to be a Pollyanna or was that natural?"

She smiled. "I think I was more like Annie with the curly red hair."

He laughed. "I love your hair." He reached out and brushed some of her wet locks away from her neck. Her flesh tingled in response.

The air felt thick between them. She wanted to tell him all the things she loved about him, but he drew his fingers back and said quickly, "So, learned or born response? The positivity?"

"Probably both. My parents are super positive, but I guess as a little girl I was a spoiled little grump."

"I don't believe it."

"Ask my parents."

"I just might."

The thought of him talking to her parents made her happy. Had they just made plans past this week like they had with the surfing? "So they started calling me their 'ray of sunshine,'" she continued. "Sometimes they still call me that." She felt a sudden pang of homesickness for her parents. She was twenty-five, had her own home, and was independent, but she still saw her parents most days of the week.

"I like that," he said quietly.

Rain pattered on the tent. Did she dare hope it was getting less heavy? Her eyelids were definitely getting heavier.

"Are you tired?" he asked.

"Yes," she admitted.

"If you promise not to make fun of me, I'll sing you to sleep."

Her eyes flew open and she turned to look at him. "Are you serious?"

"I used to sing for my sister all the time when she got scared."

His sister. She would love to meet his sister but sure hoped Brit didn't only have platonic feelings for Tess.

"I'm not scared," she said. "I've got you."

"I'm glad I help you feel safe."

"I think you could protect me from just about everything, Britton Grady."

"I would." His voice dropped low and came out in an irresistible rumble. "Or die trying."

Tess felt like he was pledging his life and allegiance to her. It was silly, but in their little isolated cocoon of this tent with the rain around them and the world so far away, it felt as if Brit was her entire world, her focus, her future. If only she dared ask him why he'd gotten so spooked after that incredible kiss. If only she dared kiss him again.

He started singing in a low voice that gave her good chills, a tender song about Jesus watching over the children. She loved that this tough guy was singing to her. She ran a huge risk of falling in love with him. If only he could answer her questions. If only he would kiss her again. As she focused on his song and grew sleepier, she knew the questions and kissing might have to wait until tomorrow.

CHAPTER NINE

Brit actually slept Wednesday night with the rain tapping rhythmically on the tent and Tess sleeping next to him. He was so impressed with and drawn to her. He wanted nothing more than to pursue her, but he kept circling around how he couldn't break his promise to Kelley. He couldn't see himself ever doing that. Not without some kind of sign from heaven. He thought about Kelley's younger sister Marley who'd been with Kelley when she died. From what he'd heard, Marley had really struggled—running away from home and getting into heavy drugs. Kelley's parents felt as if they'd lost two daughters instead of one. It was heart-wrenching. He had to remember he wasn't the only one still struggling from Kelley's death.

When he woke Thursday morning, he studied Tess as she slept. Had any woman ever been so beautiful? He'd always thought he loved Kelley, but they'd been children, eighteen-year-olds who had no clue about real life and love. Tess was all woman and had dedicated her life to helping others. She was incredible.

How could he explain that he was falling for her but he'd made a promise and he had to stand by that?

He groaned and sat up.

"Hey." Tess sat up next to him.

He forced a smile and tilted his head toward the outside. "It doesn't sound like it's pouring." Only a slight drizzle hit the tent.

"That's good."

"I'll go out and search for the treasure while you rest that ankle," he said.

"Hold up now, cowboy. You can't have all the fun without me."

He chuckled. Standing, he couldn't straighten in the tent. He held out a hand. Tess stared up at him and took it. Power surged through him as he bent down and wrapped his free hand underneath her armpit, lifting her onto her feet. She put weight on her injured ankle and her face pulled into a grimace, though of course she didn't complain.

Brit couldn't handle her hurting. He tugged her toward him and supported her. The feel of her in his arms filled him with happiness. Without meaning to, he cuddled her even closer. She leaned against him.

"Sorry I'm being such a wimp," she said, glancing up at him with those beseeching, teal-colored eyes.

"I don't think you understand the meaning of 'a wimp.'"

She smiled and tilted her face up. She was right there. Brit could easily taste those soft lips again. But at what cost to his integrity? He'd promised Kelley he wouldn't fall in love again. Such a short-sighted promise. How could he prevent himself from falling in love, especially when the perfect woman was literally dropped into his life?

He softly kissed her forehead. Even that much contact

thrilled him to the core. "I'd better get exploring," he said quietly, his lips brushing her hairline. "Will you be okay?"

She nodded and her soft cheek brushed against his neck. With a few days' growth, he hoped it wasn't too rough on her skin. "It might be a bit boring without you, but I'll be fine."

He smiled down at her. "I'll get you the playing cards. Too bad they didn't think of books."

"For sure. What kind of wilderness survival company is this?"

He laughed and gently helped her to a seated position. "I'll get breakfast before I go."

He moved to unzip the tent, but her voice stopped him. "Brit, thank you."

He glanced back at her. "For taking such superb care of you?" he tried to joke.

"That, and searching for the treasure even when you don't have to." She tilted her head. "You know, you never told me what you get out of this experience. You said you don't care about the exposure."

He didn't know if he was supposed to tell her; nobody had ever said. He paused and licked his lips. How would she react?

"What is it?" she said sweetly. "Did you make some vow not to tell me?"

He cringed at the word vow, but said, "No. The truth is, Axel's assistant hired the men on my former Navy SEAL team to each escort one woman." She nodded and he said, "For half a million dollars for the week."

"A ... a half of a million dollars!" she exploded.

Brit couldn't help but laugh at the look on her face. Shocked was an understatement.

"Oh my goodness! Are you joking with me?"

"No."

"And you don't have to find anything. You just have to protect and help me?"

"That was the agreement." He hoped she wouldn't be angry, but he was starting to wonder if Tess knew how to get angry. She'd been incredible about everything that had happened to her, even his jerky behavior of kissing her then not explaining the mess he was in. What if he told her about Kelley? He'd never told anyone, not even his sister. Though, of course, Kinsley knew the reasons he wouldn't date anyone seriously were tied to Kelley. But she thought it was because he was still mourning what he'd lost. If only she knew it was much deeper than that.

"Wowzers. Ah, Brit, that makes me super happy." Her aqua-colored eyes shone.

"It does? You're not mad I don't have to find any treasure?"

"Heck no! You totally deserve a half-million dollars and more for all you've given for our country. I seriously love Axel for doing this for all of you. Super cool."

Of course Tess would respond like that. He didn't know why he'd worried about sharing it with her. "Thanks, Tess," he said quietly. His throat suddenly felt thick and he wanted to beg her to stay with him forever, but it wasn't to be for them. "I'll be right back."

He slipped out of the tent. His heart was equal parts full of warmth for her kindness and good heart and at the same time ripping apart. After this week, he'd have to stay away from her. It would be torture.

———

Brit left after breakfast, walking away in a gray drizzle of rain. He'd check back in after each loop, so it wasn't as if she'd be alone all day, but it was a bleak prospect to spend hours in a tent with a pack of playing cards. She prayed hard for her ankle to somehow heal quick and maybe for Brit to find the treasure. If he did, would he be willing to hang out with her for a couple more days? She was falling so hard and fast for him. She wished she knew what was holding him back. It could be that he thought of her as a sister, but his kiss and the looks he gave her sure didn't support that theory.

She played solitaire a dozen times, listened to the light rain on the tent, and imagined scenario after scenario of reasons why Brit couldn't let himself like her. A new thought entered. He was being paid half a million dollars simply to be here. Maybe he felt obliged to be kind to her and not tell her to stop her motor mouth but he didn't want to lead her on with false hope.

She didn't like that thought.

Closing her eyes, she tried to rest and elevate her ankle. With the wrap, it hadn't swollen much, but she would've loved some ice. The day passed slowly, the only highlights when Brit came back from each mile out and back and when they ate lunch together.

As Brit walked away after lunch, the sun peeked out. Tess took it as a good sign and hobbled around, washing their clothes and towels in the stream the best she could and hanging every-thing out to dry. She heard helicopter rotors over the sound of the waterfall. Apparently, they only flew when it was good visi-bility, which made sense. The tourists probably didn't want to pay to see clouds.

She was tempted to hobble up to the landing pad. It would be a great break to talk to people, but something held her back. Without Brit, she felt a little uneasy revealing that she was all alone here. Maybe that was silly, but she still felt it, so she went back into the tent to lay down.

She heard footsteps. Was Brit back already? Hurrying to unzip the tent, she saw a large man rifling through their supply box. He turned in surprise and she recognized the big Hawaiian, Joe.

"Hi, Joe," she said, happy to see a familiar face.

"Oh! My *wahine nani*. I didn't know I'd find you here. Are you all alone?" He searched around then looked back at her, pumping his eyebrows. "Where's Mr. Military?"

"Um ..." Unease prickled down her spine. There was a dark-ness in Joe's face that hadn't been there before. "He'll be right back."

"Um ..." He mocked her. "Where'd he go?"

She swallowed hard. "He's just ... using the bathroom."

Joe tilted his head as if listening and then said, "Nah. You're lying to me, my *nani*." He scorned her with a big smile as he walked closer. "I don't think he will be right back. I think I've got you *all* alone." His grin turned savage. "And now you're going to tell me ... Where's the treasure, *wahine nani*?"

"What?" She didn't want to be pinned in the tent with him coming at her. She stood and shuffled to the side of the open tent door.

Unfortunately, with her ankle she couldn't move very fast. He grabbed her, yanked her against him, and pinned her arms to her sides. "I overheard Kaleo talking to boss man last night about you and Mr. Military finding treasure. Where is it? You tell me and I'll pass up my chance to have my way with you."

Horror rushed through her. How far away was Brit? Too far, she feared. He'd probably only left fifteen minutes ago, but

Kaleo had to be close by. The waterfall might drown the sound of her scream, but she had to try. "Help!" she cried out.

Joe clamped his hand over her mouth and grinned even wider. "Mr. Military's nowhere around and Kaleo's up right close to the waterfall playing tour guide. The falls are too loud to hear your scream. Where's the treasure?" His dark eyes turned hard. She'd thought he was a cute, fun guy a few days ago. There was nothing cute or fun about him now. "I've only got a few minutes. Give it to me and I won't hurt you. I'll get on the helicopter and then I'll disappear and everything will be good for you. Where is it?"

She tried to speak against his hand, but he was pushing too hard.

"If I move my hand, you'll tell me where the treasure is?" He said this in the way someone would tell a child exactly what to do if they didn't want an awful punishment.

She tried to nod, even though they had no treasure. Her mind scrambled. If she could lead him to the stream, maybe Kaleo or somebody from the waterfall group would see them and come to her aid. If she held him off with a wild goose chase, maybe he'd run out of time before the helicopter was supposed to leave. Or even better, Brit would come back.

She was panting from fear and his hand cutting off her oxygen. She prayed fervently in her mind for some kind of help or idea or the most ideal thing, for Brit to come. Panic pressed in, making her feel unsteady and lightheaded. It hadn't been long enough for Brit to have travelled the mile and back.

Joe slowly pulled his hand back a fraction. She took in a breath of air and said in a rush, "I hurt my ankle, so Brit went out to search for more treasure alone today." She was terrified to tell him there was no treasure.

Joe looked down at her wrapped ankle and then nodded. "So where is the treasure you've already found?"

"We keep it in the stream," she rushed out.

"Why?" His brow squiggled and she knew he wasn't going to buy this story.

Her mind scrambled for some reason they would keep it in the stream. She shrugged and talked fast around the stupidest lie she'd ever told. "It's diamonds." His eyes glinted at this. "They're, um, rough-cut diamonds. Brit had some silly superstition from his time in Afghanistan that if you put rough-cut diamonds in moving stream water, they'll get polished and be worth more. Worth almost as much as a cut diamond."

He blinked down at her. "That's stupid."

"I know." She managed a fake little laugh. "I didn't argue with him. He's a lot stronger than me."

"Show me." Joe started dragging her toward the stream.

Tess gasped in pain as she stepped wrong on her ankle. Joe grunted, wrapped her up tighter, and lifted her into his side and off the ground, rushing for the stream. She hated being held by him, especially with the awful threat he'd put out there.

They made it to the stream quick and he set her on her feet. She winced but didn't cry out. Looking up the river toward the waterfall, she realized the stream's path veered slightly. She could see the helicopter, but she couldn't see the edges of the waterfall pool or any people. The vegetation was too thick. Shoot. She'd have to distract Joe and then run and scream. Hopefully someone could hear her over the rushing water.

"Where is it?" Joe demanded.

She knelt down next to the stream and started lifting rocks. "We hid a sack of them under one of these big, flat rocks." She'd never thought of herself as a liar, but he seemed to believe her.

Her heart was beating so fast it was a wonder she could talk at all. Her hands quivered as she moved another rock.

Joe knelt next to her and started shoving rocks out of the way. She edged a little bit up the stream, pretending to look for the treasure. He kept shoving at rocks, looking completely distracted and enamored at the thought of finding uncut diamonds.

She said a prayer for strength and protection, hoping her ankle would hold up, and then she pushed to her feet and sprinted up the side of the stream toward the waterfall. Her ankle hurt like crazy, but it didn't collapse under her.

"Hey!" Joe roared.

She heard him behind her and she screamed as loud as she could, "Help!"

Joe tackled her from behind. She landed face-first in the mud next to the stream, crying out in pain as rocks and twigs stabbed her. Joe's huge body smothered her. She was going to suffocate, or he was going to rape or kill her. Icy horror rushed through her as he breathed into her ear, "If there aren't any diamonds, I'm going to rip you apart."

She prayed desperately, but nobody from the waterfall appeared to have heard her scream.

"Tell the truth," Joe yelled against her head, his body weight making it impossible to catch a full breath.

"If you hurt me," she gasped, "Brit will kill you."

He gave a roar of anger and wrapped his hands around her throat. "Won't matter to you because you'll be dead."

Tess's oxygen supply was already low with this massive man on top of her, but now it was cut off completely. She tried to thrash and fight, but Joe didn't budge. She prayed desperately, but as darkness edged in on her vision, she didn't have much hope. She wasn't afraid to meet her maker, but there was so much she wanted to do, so many children and families to help, and above all ...

Brit! Her mind screamed his name.

She was falling in love with him. She wanted to have the chance to at least tell him that.

She heard footsteps and then a loud, deep yell. It was almost primeval, like the armies of heaven descending in righteous fury.

Joe cursed. His hands released their grip on her and his body was flung off of her. Tess rolled onto her side, dragging in painful but blessed breaths of air and clutching at her neck.

Brit slammed into Joe and drove him into the ground. They rolled around like wild boars, grunting and slugging and wrestling it out. Fresh horror rolled through her as she watched the vicious fight. Brit was tough, big, and strong, but Joe was massive. She knew from her unfortunate encounter with him that very little of it was fat.

Joe pinned Brit to the ground. Tess screamed. Her throat was raw and the scream hurt, but she couldn't hold in even more cries as Joe slammed his meaty hands into Brit's head.

Brit bucked him off and drove his fists into Joe's abdomen, driving him back on the muddy ground. Tess's hopes rose again. Brit was so strong, but Joe wasn't done fighting. He sprung at Brit like an enraged bear and they slammed into the ground again, rolling around. Brit delivered hard blows, but Joe hardly seemed fazed.

Brit managed to squirm free for a brief second and delivered a vicious blow to Joe's temple. Joe looked stunned and Tess prayed he might be down for the count. Brit scrambled behind the larger man, locked his elbow around his throat, and pulled tight with his other arm. Joe gasped and choked for air, hitting and scratching at Brit's arms, trying to pull them away from his neck. He thrashed and tried to get free, but Brit held fast, his face a mask of determination.

Finally, Joe's body relaxed and then slumped. Brit immediately released him. He stood, looking more heroic and incredible than any superhero on any movie she'd ever seen.

He looked at her and the anger and determination faded in an instant. "Tess," he breathed out her name.

She stood on shaky legs. Her ankle hurt but it supported her. Brit crossed the distance in quick strides and swept her off the ground. He stared at her as if she was his world. She probably shouldn't have done it, but in the intensity of the moment, she wrapped her arms around his neck and kissed him. She kissed him hard and long, and he returned it. The kiss was intense and full of the concern he felt but also his fierce protectiveness and connection to her.

This man would do anything for her, be everything for her, love her like she'd never known was possible.

When he pulled back, they were both sucking in rapid gulps of air. He rested his forehead against hers and murmured, "Ah, Tess. Are you okay?"

"Yes," she said. Her voice was raspy.

His eyes widened and he gritted out, "He choked you."

He bent low and tenderly kissed her neck. A thrill went through her. She didn't care about the past or Joe. She only cared about Brit—more time with him, more kisses, more holding each other, and eventually talking about that tortured look she'd seen in his eyes the last time they kissed and how they were going to move past whatever was haunting him and be together.

Joe stirred and sat up. Brit immediately set her on her feet and stepped in front of her.

"Joe?" a voice called from around the bend and then Kaleo appeared. He saw them and raised a hand. "Have you two seen Joe? He disappeared and ..." His voice trailed off. He looked from Joe struggling to his feet and Brit protecting Tess. "What happened?"

Brit glared at Joe. "Joe attacked Tess, that's what happened."

Joe put his hands up and slowly stood. "Come on, brah." His voice sounded as raw as Tess's felt from Joe choking her. "You know I wouldn't attack no woman."

"Don't you dare," Brit roared. "When I came up, he had her pinned face down and he was choking her."

Kaleo's eyebrows jerked up and he looked to Tess.

"He was," she said, and her throat luckily wasn't quite as painful. "He wanted the treasure he thought we'd found and threatened to ... do bad things to me if I didn't hand it over."

"Ah, Joe, you stinking idiot," Kaleo groaned. "I worried when you overheard me talking to Mr. Dexter and I saw that greedy gleam in your eyes." He pushed out a breath. "Joe's my cousin. He's usually laidback but sometimes he flips. Loves the easy money, see? I brought him here from Maui and promised my auntie I'd keep him in work, keep him away from his rotten friends, and watch out for him. He's never served time, but we all know he's done ... things he shouldn't for money and drugs."

Brit was tense against her. "Does Axel know?"

"Nah, brah. He wouldn't have let me use Joe if he'd known." He shook his head. "Joe, you're such an idiot. I'm gonna be in a lot of trouble with Mr. Dexter. Maybe lose my contract with the helis."

Tess would've felt bad for Kaleo if she hadn't recently been attacked by Joe.

"Here's what's going to happen," Brit said in a steely voice.

"Kaleo, you will take your tourists and Joe and get out of here. I will have the police waiting for Joe at the landing pad. When we leave here Saturday, we'll talk to the police."

"No way," Joe protested. "Come on!"

Brit gave him a look and he cowered and focused on the ground. "If Joe disappears, you will be held responsible for that, Kaleo." He studied the man. Kaleo nodded; he clearly understood he couldn't aid his cousin any longer. "And if you try to disappear," Brit added, staring Joe down, "I will get my SEAL squadron together, we will find you, and you know what will happen then? Actually, it'll be your choice—dismemberment or death."

Tess flinched in surprise.

Joe pushed his toe in the dirt, saying nothing, but his hands were shaking.

"Let's go," Kaleo commanded Joe. He nodded to Tess and Brit. "I'm so sorry about what happened. You have my word he won't disappear."

Brit lifted his chin to him. He obviously wasn't ready to forgive Kaleo's involvement in this mess. She thought Kaleo would do the right thing, but the bond of family was strong, especially amongst Hawaiian families. She usually admired that, but she didn't want Joe running free if he could hurt someone else like he'd hurt her.

Joe slunk in front of Kaleo and they walked toward the landing pad for the helicopter and their waiting tourists.

Brit watched them go, then turned to her. "Tess," he murmured. He looked over her neck again and then met her gaze. "Are you sure you're okay?"

She nodded. "Thank you for saving me." The words were inadequate compared to what he'd done for her. After he called the police, she'd give him a kiss of gratitude that would leave no doubt what a hero he was to her.

He swept her off her feet and into his arms. She wanted to kiss him right here and now but she was suddenly exhausted. She lay her head in the crook of his neck and let him carry her back to their little camp. He set her in one of the camp chairs and propped her foot up on another one.

Looking her over, he asked, "Will you be okay while I call the police?"

"Yes."

"Do you want to call this week quits? We can have Kaleo fly back for us."

"No!" The word was said much too vehemently. She didn't want to give up on the treasure, but even more than that, she didn't want to give up any time with Brit.

"You're sure?"

She nodded. "I want to see it through."

He gently touched her face. "Bravest woman I know," he said quietly.

A warm quiver darted through her. She wanted him to bend down and kiss her, but something clouded his gaze, something sad, almost desperate. He gave her a conflicted smile, pulled the phone out of the backpack and made the call, walking away to talk.

Tess studied him, filled with an intense longing to be back in his safe, strong arms. As soon as he was done with the call, she was going to kiss him until he pulled away, and then they were going to talk. She'd impetuously thought she'd tell him she loved him, but was he ready to hear that? She didn't know.

But she did know one thing for sure. The treasure was important to her, but nothing was as important as Brit.

CHAPTER TEN

Brit finished his phone call. The officer he'd talked to had been great, and he'd known all about Joe Iousa, had been warned by the Maui officers and had been keeping an eye on him for a while. The detective told him how the guy was chill as anyone you'd meet, then sometimes he just flipped. Usually when it involved money. Detective Palekiko reassured Brit they would put Joe in custody as per Brit's testimony and take written and verbal statements from him and Tess when they came back Saturday night.

Brit should've felt reassured when he hung up the phone, but he was angry. He stayed facing the creek to give himself a minute to calm down. He was angry at Joe, at Kaleo, but mostly at himself. Why had he left Tess alone to search for some elusive, stupid treasure? She was the real treasure and he should never have left her. True, the treasure was for her and her charity, but he would gladly give her his massive and unnecessary paycheck so she could expand her charity. Then Brit could just hold her for the next two days.

As those tempting thoughts surfaced, another realization came like a punch in the gut. He wasn't free to hold and love her and he was the worst kind of jerk to keep leading her on. His shoulders rounded. Seeing Tess in that monster's grip, the fight with Joe, the amazing kiss with Tess, and dealing with the aftermath had pushed his own responsibilities completely from his mind.

He thought about that kiss as he stared at the water running downstream. That kiss had been more than the passion and adrenaline of the moment. It had been filled with commitment, his vow to protect Tess and to love her.

Love her.

He loved Tess, despite trying so hard not to. She was optimistic, funny, talkative, irresistible, impressive, caring, fun ... the list could go on and on in his head. Tess was everything he'd ever wanted, even though he hadn't let himself admit he'd wanted anyone. At first, he'd mourned Kelley deeply, but as the years passed, he'd wondered how he could've gotten himself into a lifelong bond to a woman who was gone.

He couldn't, and wouldn't, break his promise to Kelley. He wouldn't be able to live with himself. What was he going to do?

He said a short and empty prayer for help, then took some deep breaths as he waited for an answer that didn't come.

Pushing out a heavy breath, he turned and started toward Tess. She sat in the camp chair, gazing up at him as if he was her hero.

He was no hero. A hero wouldn't take advantage of this situation with a trusting, beautiful angel like her and kiss her so deeply and then break her heart.

He dropped to his knees in front of her and checked her ankle propped up on the chair. "Did you hurt it?" he asked, referring to her ankle.

She shook her head. "I think it's okay. Even when I ran from him, it hurt but it supported me."

"Good." He gently ran his palms up her shapely calf and she let out a soft groan of pleasure. He jolted away from her. What was he doing? He couldn't seem to resist touching her and he ached to just hold her and reassure himself she was all right. He had to stop those desires in their tracks before they consumed him.

Pushing to his feet, he paced away and then started talking, but didn't allow himself to look at her. "The police detective seemed like a great guy. They'll take Joe into custody, but we'll have to go file a report before we fly home Saturday."

"Okay," she said.

What else could he talk about besides admitting he was falling in love with her, but he was the jerk of all jerks and needed to stay far away from her? He wasn't sure how staying away would be possible. Not for the next two days. He looked at their small tent. Last night, he'd done pretty well after her prayer. Tonight, he was afraid he'd pull her in close and kiss the night away. The remembrance of their kisses was too strong.

He drummed his fist against his thigh and kept walking and talking. "So I found another clue today."

"What did it say?" she asked. He could tell, could hear it in her voice she was confused and frustrated, wondering what was going on, why he wasn't holding her and comforting her like he ached to do.

"Your treasure will make you happy for a lifetime." He stopped walking and let himself look at her. She was so beautiful, those twists of red and deep brown hair, the teal-blue eyes, the lips ...

Dang, man, don't look at her lips.

She shook her head and said, "Do you think there is even a treasure? Is Axel just a twisted billionaire who's having a great time laughing at us?"

He laughed. She was incredible. "Come on, where's my ray of sunshine?"

Shoot, had he really just said that?

"You're right. Sorry." She focused on her clenched hands. "That was lame of me. I'm still a little shaken up from Joe's attack and not sure what to think or do right now."

Brit was drawn to her like a moth to flame. But this beautiful flame wouldn't burn him, only make him break a promise. "What can I do to help?"

She looked up, wet her lips, and asked in the sweetest voice he'd ever heard, "Can you please just hold me?"

The oxygen was ripped from his lungs. Brit had no power to resist that request. He bent low, scooped her out of the chair and held her against his chest. He felt so strong and powerful with her in his arms. He could conquer the world. At the same time, he was weak for her, and he wanted to be weak for her for the rest of eternity.

What was happening to him? How had he allowed this to happen?

Now that it had, he was powerless to let her go. Just for a moment, he'd hold her and comfort her. She needed him. It was selfless. He almost gave a disgruntled laugh. There was nothing selfless about him wanting to hold her day and night.

He sank into the camp chair her foot had been resting on and cuddled her in close. She sighed and lay her head on his chest. She wrapped one arm around his shoulder, her other hand trapped between them. His breath came in short bursts. He had never felt anything as incredible as holding the woman who exceeded any dream of his perfect woman. A dream he'd never allowed himself to dwell on.

He let his hands wander along her back and her waist. She felt so perfect. Slow, wonderful minutes passed as he simply held her. He'd love to kiss her again but knew he'd be sunk if he did. She'd asked him to hold her and he couldn't have refused that request. She needed him. It didn't mean he was going to let himself love her and break his promise, though he wasn't sure he'd be strong enough to refuse her if she told him she loved him.

She burrowed in closer. He felt her body tremble and then wetness on his neck. He pulled back abruptly and stared down at her. "You're crying? Did I make you cry?"

"No." She shook her head and brushed at the wetness on her cheeks. "It's just all the emotions coming to the surface. Being so terrified when Joe had me pinned down and choked me, being so grateful and overwhelmed when you came and beat him, then aching for you to hold me close but you got distant again and I was afraid you were going to push me away. I've never been a needy person, ever, but ... I need you, Brit."

She blinked up at him, irresistible, perfect, appealing, every good thing he wanted. She needed him. An industrial crane couldn't have pulled him away at that moment. She wound her arms around his neck, pulled herself closer, and kissed him.

Heaven help him, he didn't hesitate to kiss her back. He pushed all rational thought away as the kiss took over his brain and his body.

The kiss started out needy, emotional, with almost a desperation to be close and never be pulled apart. Brit felt the kiss change to a sharing of commitment and joy that was unparalleled. He'd never leave Tess's side. No one could ever pull them apart.

As he deepened the kiss and savored this incredible connection and a depth of feeling he'd never thought possible in this lifetime, his brain finally caught up with his lips and hands and pleasure receptors. He wasn't free to commit to Tess. He was already committed to Kelley, and would be until he died.

A heavy, overwhelming depression settled on him. He forced himself to break the kiss. He wanted to hold Tess close, to comfort and care for her, but he wasn't strong enough to draw lines in the sand. When she was in his arms, he was weak, needy. He had no self-control, no sense of honor.

She smiled sweetly up at him, but her smile immediately slipped when she saw his face. "You've got that tortured look in your eyes again," she said softly.

"Oh, Tess," he groaned out her name and clung to her when he should be running the other direction. "I'm so sorry." He clamped his jaw and then admitted, "I can't do this."

"This?" Her beautiful gaze searched his and then she swirled her finger between the two of them. "This meaning us?"

He nodded, sure his eyes were every bit as tortured as he felt inside. He flexed his quads and stood with her in his arms. Carefully setting her in the other chair, he gently lifted her injured leg onto the chair they'd been in, then took to pacing in front of her. She simply watched him, not moving to touch him or stop him. Luckily. As he'd proven time and again, he had no control with her in his arms and especially not when she pressed her lips to his.

She said nothing, which surprised him, but he appreciated

her silence. He didn't know what to say, how to tell her why he was such a mess. She had an unbelievably great attitude, despite everything that happened to her, but he didn't think she would keep letting him off the hook. He'd kissed her—or rather returned her kiss—three beautiful times now, desperately kissed her. He wanted to gush like a tough military man never gushed about how great she was, but that would only confuse her more.

Finally, he stopped pacing and glanced at her, then focused on the creek babbling by. "I'll make us some dinner," he managed.

"Brit?" The sweetness of his name on her lips brought his gaze back to her.

They locked gazes and the world fell away. He felt energized and renewed, but trepidation also filtered in. She would demand answers. She had every right to.

"Thank you for being here for me."

Brit could only nod and turn toward the supplies. His chest was tight and pain rippled through him, making his shoulders heave. What was he doing leading Tess on like this? He needed to stop or he'd hurt her even worse. He was a stupid, insensitive jerk to both Kelley and Tess.

Brit warmed up the chicken alfredo and broccoli dinners. Tess moved her injured leg off the chair, despite his protests, and they ate in silence. The waterfall spilled merrily not too far away and there were birds chirping and small creatures scurrying in the undergrowth, but between the two of them, it was just this … unfulfilled silence. Tess didn't make it awkward; she didn't even act mad at him. He cleaned up dinner and she stood, brushing her teeth. He did the same.

It wasn't even dark yet. If only they could go swim. He'd carry her up there and then hold her in the water. He mentally slapped himself. No carrying her. No holding her. Especially no kissing her. He passed a hand over his face. None of his men would believe it if they knew what a mess he was. The pastors he'd talked to would believe it, but even with those trusted authorities, he'd never shared the real truth.

He focused on the here and now. What was he going to do tomorrow? He didn't dare leave her again to search for the treasure, but he felt duty-bound to find it for her. He could only imagine what she'd say if he tried to give her his money. He pushed out a harsh laugh. He was also duty-bound to love no one but Kelley, and that wasn't working out so well, was it?

"Brit?" Tess questioned all innocent and sweet.

He looked over at her. She was holding on to a nearby tree and semi-balancing on one foot. She was so beautiful and he knew she could never be his. It hurt to look at her.

"Are you okay?" she asked.

Brit grunted out a breath of disgust. "No, I'm not okay. I'm a complete mess and this is so unfair to you and ... I'm sorry, Tess. I'm sorry for my lack of self-control and I'm sorry for sending you conflicting messages and I'm sorry that I keep kissing you when I shouldn't."

She stared at him and then said in a quiet voice, "You regret kissing me?"

"Of course I regret kissing you." The words were out before he could pull them back and she flinched as if he'd hit her. "Oh, Tess." He pushed at his hair. "Not like that." He held up both hands, beseeching her. "I have absolutely loved every second of the kisses and touches we shared. It's not about the kisses. It's not you. I'm just ... a mess."

The pain around her eyes eased a little bit. "Can you tell me about it?"

He stared at her. Tell her about it? Confess that he'd given his heart away at eighteen and it had been buried with Kelley because of the stupid promise he'd made? He hadn't told anyone. His parents, his sister, his men, the Navy therapists, the pastors and preachers he'd talked to. He'd never admitted to any of them what he'd promised or why he couldn't move on with his life. They all assumed it was PTSD from his many tours and battles. He hadn't told them because he didn't want their platitudes and sympathy. He especially didn't want someone to tell him he shouldn't be bound to a promise like that for life. He'd done it and he had to stand by it. He'd asked Kelley not to do it— begged, really—but she had feistily declared her solemn vow on the Holy Bible. She'd been so innocent and in love with him; how could he not vow the same? They'd both assumed that if one of them died, it would be him, and she'd live the tragic love story she'd created. When the tables had turned ... he had to stand by it. There was no other option.

As he gazed at the perfect and amazing woman in front of him, he searched his mind and prayed for another option. *Please, Lord. Please, Kelley. Please, someone help me know how to love Tess and somehow not break my promise to Kelley.* Being with Tess was all he wanted now and he couldn't imagine that changing anytime soon.

"I don't know how to tell you about it," he finally admitted.

Tess pursed her lips, staring at him, and then the quiet she'd maintained for the past hour broke in a flood. "I'm going absolutely insane, Brit. Like out of my mind." She shook her dark-red curls irresistibly. "You kiss me like we're Romeo and Juliet and I love every second of your touch, even better your kiss, but I don't want some romantic fatalistic story. I want you in my life, every day, every minute."

Brit swallowed hard and found himself having to blink at the sudden, horrific moisture in his eyes. All they could be was a tragic romance. Worse than him and Kelley. It was crazy because he shouldn't feel this close to and connected with Tess, but if he was honest with himself, he loved her like he'd never loved Kelley. And he had to leave her. It was awful, but he didn't see another solution.

"Can you please tell me what's going on?"

He wanted to, but this secret had been hidden for so long that he didn't know how to let it out. He prayed that she wouldn't hate him.

"Maybe if I guess?" She started rattling off reasons before he could respond. "You're only allowed to date supermodels or actresses because you're the most perfect man in creation, so you need someone equal to you in looks."

He grunted out a disgusted laugh. "No, and you are much more beautiful than any supermodel or actress."

She put a hand to her heart. "Oh, that was sweet. You're silly and obviously have a skewed perception, but I appreciate the kind words." He wanted to tell her he wasn't silly or skewed. She was gorgeous. She rushed on before he could say a word. "You're only allowed to date CEOs, doctors, lawyers, or influencers because of how impressive and brave you are and you need someone equal to you in impressiveness."

He looked her over. "You're more impressive than any woman I know, and again," he had to spit it out quick before she started talking, "more beautiful."

Her lip trembled. "Thank you again." She sighed and pursed her lips, then said, "Oh, I've got it." She snapped her fingers. "You made a vow of celibacy when you were in the military."

"No. Isn't that monks?" Despite the anguish rolling through him, he found himself smiling slightly. Her guess was very close.

"You made a promise to your Navy SEAL buddies that you'd never fall for a redhead?"

He actually laughed. "No. They'd all tell me to date you." He looked over her beautiful face and shape, knowing that her inside was a million times more beautiful than her outside. "They'd definitely approve of you ... or try to steal you."

"I didn't know you were such a sweet talker."

He guffawed. "I'm not."

She only raised her eyebrows and kept guessing. "You're opposed to long-distance relationships."

"No." More like unable to form any relationship at all.

Her shoulders slumped. "I'm running out of ideas. Hmm." He watched her think and wished he could think clearly himself. Should he tell her? What would her response be? Would telling her be more merciful than leading her on and making her guess? He didn't know. In four days, he'd not only fallen in love, but felt close enough to her that he thought he could share the secret he'd shared with no one.

She looked into his eyes and her own filled with sadness and yet wonder. "You were deeply in love with someone and she died and broke your heart and now you know you can never find a love like that again."

Brit sucked in a breath, shocked at how close she was to the truth. "I'm right, aren't I?" she asked. "No one can compare to your first, lost love."

"Tess, please ..." He looked away. "I haven't told anyone about this."

"No one?" The disbelief in her voice got him to look at her.

"No one."

She jutted out her chin and her eyes flashed to an almost blue color. He waited for her to get mad at him, but instead she said, "You hardly know me, Brit. You don't have to tell me if you don't want to."

He felt a moment's reprieve at her kindness. She wouldn't force him to tell her, but somehow, he would spit it out. First, he had to say, "You're wrong, Tess." The words came out vehemently.

She leaned back and asked, "About?"

"I do know you." He swallowed hard and admitted, "I know your incredible attitude, your busy tongue that never stops and makes me smile, your happy sunshine that blesses me and I'm sure everyone around you, your brilliant mind that spins thinking how to make the world better for others, your beautiful face and body and smile and those eyes that I want to stare into the rest of my life. I know you, Tess." His voice got deep and husky. "And I love everything I know about you."

"Brit ..." Her voice was filled with awe and a love that made his heart race. "I don't know what to say. I wish I could kiss you right now."

His voice got even huskier as he looked at her tempting mouth. "Believe me, Tess, the feeling is completely mutual."

She smiled and he almost ran and swept her into his arms. He clenched his fists instead, wishing for the millionth time that he knew what to do. The obstacle between them was right there, a brick wall between them, with no way around it. At least she knew how he felt about her. He never wanted her thinking she was less or that she lacked anything and that was the reason he wouldn't cave to her irresistible appeal.

Half a minute went by and then she asked, "Would you mind carrying me up to the waterfall pool? I'd love to wash off after everything that happened with Joe and not being able to take a bath last night."

Brit was stunned by her request. Once again, she wasn't pushing him or pinning him down. She was incredible. He wanted nothing more than to carry her to that pool and kiss her and hold her all night. He stared at her, torn and more in love than he'd ever been.

CHAPTER ELEVEN

Tess studied Brit. His sweet, tender words kept rolling through her mind. Could this amazing man truly love everything about her? She was a little out of touch in the bubble of her charity and her online world, but he was the best man she'd ever known. Absolutely perfect to her. She wasn't perfect, but Brit seemed to think she was.

Ah, Brit. She would never forget the beautiful things he'd just said and most especially his husky voice as he'd admitted, "Believe me, Tess, the feeling is completely mutual." He wanted to kiss her. He'd been as floored by their kisses as she had.

If only she knew exactly what was holding him back. As soon as she'd mentioned the woman he loved dying, his face had gotten that tortured look again. Tess wanted to know everything, most especially if she could ever fill his heart like the woman he'd lost obviously had. It was torture knowing he'd loved someone so deeply that he couldn't move on.

What made Tess think she was something special? What

made her think she could help him heal from his lost love and move on? Move on with her?

Was she out of line to ask him to carry her to the waterfall? Yes, she wanted him to hold her, wanted to be close to him, but she also wanted to baby her ankle tonight and hopefully be able to get out and search with him for the treasure tomorrow. They were running out of time to help her children, but also running out of time to be together. She was going to savor every minute because she had an awful feeling in her gut that she might not see him again after they parted ways Saturday.

Brit's eyes looked unsettled and agonized, but he only nodded and said, "Of course I'll carry you to the waterfall. Washing off sounds great."

She smiled her gratitude. He walked to her, his gaze intense. Each step illustrated how beautifully he was built, how appealing he was. He scooped her up and her arms naturally went around his neck. Brit's breathing became ragged and she felt her own do the same. She had a stitch in her chest and wanted to kiss him so badly it hurt.

Glancing up into his handsome face, she asked, "Is this going to be okay?"

He stared down at her. "No, Tess. It's not."

Pain rippled through her. "You can set me down. I can hobble my way to the waterfall."

A brief smile broke through his anguish and he said, "Sorry, I misunderstood. I thought you meant you and I. I can carry you to the waterfall."

He started walking on the path they'd created along the creek. Did he realize that him meaning *they* wouldn't be okay was far worse than him not being able to handle carrying her? They wouldn't work. She didn't feel that she should demand answers from him, but the pain of his certainty that they could never work ... it was an awful reality she didn't know if she could face.

She might not get many more chances to cling to him, so she lay her head in the crook of his neck and felt his pulse racing against her forehead. She loved him. Without a doubt. And he couldn't love her back. Maybe this was what that old eighties rock song had meant by "Hurts so good." Every touch and look between them felt like exquisite torture.

He made it to the pool and set her on her feet, then bent down to take off his shoes and socks. She wanted to wait and make him carry her again, but instead she slipped off her flip flops and carefully waded into the pool. Her ankle was doing all right. When she was thigh deep, she heard him coming in behind her. She laid back in the water, kicking to stay afloat.

She assumed he'd swim to the waterfall and try to stay away from her. When she felt his warm palms underneath her upper back and thighs, she jolted in surprise. Blinking her eyes open, she stared into his dark gaze, lifting her head slightly out of the water. She hoped to hear some declaration of his love and how he'd work through whatever he couldn't tell her about the love he'd lost.

Instead, he said, "Shall we unwrap your ankle and then you can float and see how it feels? I can wrap it up again tonight."

"Oh ... that'd be good."

His gaze trailed over her face and then he stunned her again, muttering, "Hold on to me and I'll unwrap it for you."

Tess had no problem complying. She wrapped her arms around his bare, perfect back and clung to him as he unwrapped the dressing. Once it was free, he wadded it and threw it to the bank by their shoes. Tess should probably let go of him, but he put his hands under her back and thighs again and encouraged her, "Now you can float."

"Thanks," she murmured.

He nodded, much too serious. Whatever was weighing on him was dreadfully heavy. If only she could take the pain and anguish from him. She'd do anything to help him.

Closing her eyes, she enjoyed the feeling of weightlessness, of his hands supporting her. It was nice to have the wrap off her ankle and just lay in the water with her hair floating around her. She tried to not worry, just let it all go and be weightless in mind as well as body for at least a minute, but she couldn't do it. She cared far too much for Brit to just let her worries go.

Opening her eyes, she stared up at him. His gaze was concentrated on her face. When she met his eyes, he startled but then settled quickly. Their gazes got tangled up and a world of understanding, hurt, regret, and impossible wishes passed between them. She could almost believe he'd fallen for her just like she'd fallen for him. Maybe she was reading too much into his glance. If the love of his life had really died, how could she compete with an angel? Of course the woman would be immortalized in his mind. Maybe Tess could never measure up.

She could've stared into his eyes all evening, but her ears started hurting from being submersed in the water. She lifted her head and dropped her legs. He let her go. She stood in the water. Her ankle didn't hurt since there wasn't pressure on it, but her heart hurt something fierce. She and Brit couldn't be together and she didn't even know the complete story.

They stood there, staring at each other as the sun set to the west. When Brit opened his mouth, she thought he'd say they should go get some rest, but instead he said in a deep, inspiring tone, "I would give anything in the world to kiss you again."

Tess's heart walloped against her chest. She wanted to tease, trick, or cajole him into it, but she feared the woman he'd loved still held his heart. Maybe his guilt at wanting to kiss Tess was overwhelming him. Instead of kissing him like she wanted, she said, "But you've got too much honor to do that, don't you?"

His fists clenched and his jaw got rock hard. "I don't know about that. I didn't have too much honor the last three times I kissed you."

She raised her eyebrows. "I don't know if your memory is lapsing, but I kissed you, every single time." Her face flared with heat as she realized that was true. Every single time, she had kissed him, not the other way around.

A tortured smile slipped across his face. "I don't know if your memory is lapsing, but I kissed you back, and I loved it, every single time."

She smiled, grateful for him once again reminding her that he did care, that he was taken by her, even if he couldn't allow himself to be with her. It seemed someone else already had full claim on his heart. As that awful thought hit her, a tear crested her eyelid and rolled down her cheek.

Brit's body tensed and he said in a gravelly voice, "The thought of me not kissing you first makes you cry."

She wanted to cry harder, but she released a frustrated laugh instead. "No. The thought of never kissing you again makes me cry."

"Ah, Tess." Brit reached up and cupped her face with his palm.

The tears came hard and fast then. She couldn't seem to stop them once they started spilling out. She had never considered herself a crier, but the thought of losing Brit before she really had him made her entire body wrench in pain. The moisture associated with that agony squeezed out her eyes as if they were the only escape hatch.

"Tess," Brit groaned. He tugged her to him and enfolded her in his strong arms.

She had no strength or desire to resist. Her tears didn't slow as she buried her face in the warm flesh of his chest and let the cry session run its course. Brit held her as if it would be the last time he touched her.

The night deepened around them as they clung to each other. Her tears slowed and then stopped. She'd give anything to tilt up her face and kiss him, taste his mouth one more time, feel the urgency and the love he had for her.

She couldn't allow herself to do it. She had kissed him every time, and it made her love him even more that he was too honorable to instigate a kiss with her. Yes, he'd kissed her back, but that also deepened her love for him. Those kisses had been every bit as powerful for him as they had for her, and even with his deep sense of honor, he hadn't been able to stop himself from kissing her back. She couldn't put him in a position where he felt he was breaking his honor again. He was so good. If only she could stop guessing about some perfect woman he'd loved and lost and know for sure what had created the wall between them. But maybe it would be worse to know the complete story. It must be of the utmost importance to him or Brit wouldn't let it come between them. She knew that as surely as she knew she never wanted to leave his arms.

His lips tenderly brushed her forehead and he whispered as if hesitant to break their connection. "We'd better get some rest."

"Okay," was all she could manage. Her friends and family would be shocked. Tess was never without words.

Brit swooped her up into his arms and pushed through the

water, carrying her to the edge. He set her down so he could shove his shoes on and she could slide into her flip flops. Then he picked her up again and carried her through the darkness back to camp. This little spot felt like home. She wanted a home with Brit. She felt tears prick her eyes again. She needed to stop thinking things like that and getting all weepy about it.

Brit gently set her in the camp chair and re-wrapped her ankle, then helped her into the tent so she could change. He changed outside.

When they were both in dry clothes, they settled onto their separate sleeping pads without either of them saying a word. Tess felt like Brit was churning things over in his mind. She wanted him to share with her, but she was scared to hear it at the same time.

"Can we pray together?" she asked into the silence.

"I would love that," he answered.

They both knelt and she was amazed that her ankle felt pretty good. If only her heart could feel the same.

"I'll say it," he offered.

"Okay. Thanks."

She bowed her head and folded her arms tightly.

Brit thanked the Lord for their protection and beseeched Him to watch over their families. He thanked Him for this opportunity to be together and then his voice dropped low and he said, "And please bless me to know how to share with Tess and bless her to know that she's the most incredible person I've ever known. Amen."

Tess echoed the amen, feeling off kilter and full of anticipation. He was going to tell her. Her heart raced with nerves and the desire to get it over with. If it was as bad as Brit acted ... she should probably kiss him one last time before he told her and she was also honor-bound not to act on her desire. She edged closer, a thrill rushing through her at the thought of surprising him with a last kiss, but he started talking before she could.

"I need to tell you, Tess."

"Okay," she said, her voice squeaking with fear as she eased back, missing out on the chance of another kiss. Fear and disappointment settled in her gut like a rock.

They sat on opposite sides of the small tent. There wasn't much distance between them, but it felt like miles.

Brit's voice was hoarse and filled with pain as he began, "When I was a junior in high school, I fell in love. Her name was Kelley."

Was? So his angel had died. Tess wrapped her arms around her legs and clung to them.

"We dated for almost two years. When I came back from boot camp the summer after graduation, before I got my first assignment with the Navy, she sat me down and she swore to me, on a Holy Bible to boot ..." He let out a frustrated and strangled grunt. "She swore that if I died, she would never love again. She'd die alone."

Tess could see exactly where this tragic story was going, the loss Axel had talked about. She already hated the ending.

His voice got raspier. "I tried to talk her out of it, assuming I'd probably be killed since I planned to be in the Navy for at least eight to ten years and I wanted to be a SEAL. There was no talking her out of it. We were eighteen and, in her mind, it was this show of devotion and love that she'd tragically live a long, lonely life and die without love if something happened to me."

Tess's tongue was frozen. She had no response to the scratchy silence that settled over the tent.

He continued even more quietly, but she could unfortunately

still hear him. "After she swore her oath, I knew I had no choice but to return it. So I promised that if she died, I'd never love again and I'd die alone. As an eighteen-year-old, thinking I was going to death or glory in the military, the thought of *her* dying and me being alone never crossed my mind. I thought the entire solemn vow was this selfless act on her part. I never could've imagined that a few months after I left Cedar Hills ... she'd be killed in a car accident."

Tess sucked in a breath. She clung to her knees and rocked slowly. What on earth could she say? She wanted to reach out to him, to comfort him, but she couldn't. He'd made a vow as an eighteen-year-old that had changed his life.

Never love again . . . Die alone . . .

Her heart felt like it shriveled and died right along with his and Kelley's.

She could completely understand how that poor girl would've loved Brit so deeply to promise she'd never love again. Brit and Kelley had been young, but they'd dated for two years and had probably grown very close. Brit was the best man in creation, so of course Kelley would love him desperately. Tess had only known him four days and already she loved him like she'd never imagined she could love someone. If he died, she'd want to be alone. But selfishly, she wanted him to love her more than he'd loved Kelley and to break his promise.

She closed her eyes. She could never ask that of him. No wonder Tess had been the one to initiate their kisses. No wonder he'd had such a tortured look in his eyes at times. No wonder he couldn't love Tess.

Any dreams she'd had of the two of them being together disappeared like leaves swirled away in a vicious windstorm. She had no idea what to say or do to make it better. Probably because there was no way to make this better.

Long minutes ticked by. She didn't know how long—time and reality were cruel masters that she hated right now. The air was stuffy and heavy in the tent.

Finally, Brit said, "Please say something, Tess."

Even at this crucial, awful moment, she realized how much she loved when he said her name. But she had nothing to say to him, nothing that would make this any better.

"I'm so sorry, Brit," she managed through her thick, scratchy throat.

He heaved out a loud breath and then murmured, "Me too." He waited as if giving her the chance to say more.

She had nothing. No words of comfort, inspiration, or hope. For the first time in a long time, she felt as depressed and unhappy as if she'd lost every person that mattered to her.

Eventually, he stretched out on his bed. She did the same. She could hear him breathe and it definitely wasn't slow and easy as if he was sleeping. She doubted she'd sleep either. Her mind turned his words and his vow and their situation over and over again. She couldn't see any solution.

Brit was going to die alone and without love.

So was she.

CHAPTER TWELVE

The next morning dawned cloudy again. Brit knew he'd fallen asleep at some point, but it had been troubled. He'd had awful dreams about Kelley and Tess being in a car together and slamming into a barricade. When he reached them, they were both covered in blood and dead.

He and Tess didn't talk much as they got ready to look for the treasure. He should try to convince her to stay in camp, but he was loathe to leave her. He couldn't imagine the trauma she'd experienced being attacked by Joe and he couldn't stand to think of her sitting here fearing that or stewing over what he'd revealed last night. She kept saying her ankle was okay and she wanted to go. Her sunny disposition was definitely gone—he could blame himself for that—but she still had her determination and grit. He admired her even more than his own mom and sister. That was really saying something.

They set out and traversed mile after mile, slowly, without finding anything. As they were almost ready to be done for the evening, he saw something semi-hidden under some bushes. Stopping, he reached down and grabbed it. Turning to Tess, he had a sinking feeling it was only another note.

"Do you want to open it?" he asked.

"You do the honors," she said with a forced smile. He really missed her talking nonstop to him.

He searched through the gift wrap and found the note. "Your treasure will change everything."

Tess rolled her eyes and clenched and then popped her fingers. "Mind ... blown. Do you think Axel had his five-year-old nephew come up with these earth-shattering clues? Of course the treasure will change everything."

Brit chuckled. He couldn't help it. "Axel's an only child," he said.

She lifted her eyebrows and nodded. "He must still be a child at heart."

He laughed again, liking the release of it. "Definitely." He put the note in his backpack, took a drink of his water, and asked, "Are you getting fed up with it?"

Her face froze and he knew immediately she thought he was referring to the tension and awkwardness between them.

"Us not finding anything," he clarified. For some reason, he glanced at the camera she wore. How much of their relationship would be displayed for the world? If his sister saw any of it, she'd hound him until he talked and then there would be two women alive who knew about his fatalistic promise. Up to this point he'd only dodged her yanking the truth out of him because they were rarely in the same state.

"Oh ... I'm trying to keep my spirits up. Maybe tomorrow Axel will give me the consolation prize. Here's a hundred dollars for finding all the notes but none of the treasure."

"There's the spirit." He tilted his head and studied her. She was so beautiful and he just wanted to touch her cheek. He lifted his hand but dropped it quickly when her eyes widened. Now that she knew the truth about him, did she think he was an out of control loser for kissing her so passionately when he was supposed to have locked his heart for a lifetime?

"How's your ankle?" he asked instead.

"Pretty good. It hurts, but not too bad."

"Would you tell me if it was bad? My ray of sunshine?" He'd meant to joke, referring to her parents' name for her, but calling her "his" was no joke.

She nodded very seriously. "I would tell you. I'm okay. You ready to head back?"

"Yeah."

They walked quietly back, ate dinner in silence, and then went to the waterfall to wash off. As Tess plunged in, Brit couldn't keep his gaze from her. She went under and came up and her hair was plastered to her head. Her smooth face had water running down it and her clothes clung to her beautiful curves.

Brit splashed some water on his face and looked away when she glanced at him. He was an absolute mess. He wished his sister Kinsley was here to make fun of him and tease him out of this morose state. She wasn't here, so he just got angry inside. He wanted to curse Axel for putting him in this situation and then curse himself worse for letting his feelings, and Tess's, get so deep. If he had any semblance of self-control, he wouldn't be in this state—fighting the urge to scream out to the trees and the waterfall and most importantly to Tess that he loved her. Then he'd grab her and kiss her and never stop. Heaven. That's what kissing her again would be.

He let his eyes wander her direction. She was floating on her back again. Brit wanted to go hold her like last night, but he had to stay away or he would break. It had been a miracle he hadn't caved last night.

Brit swam to the waterfall and around for a bit, then floated on his back. He treaded water and caught her staring at him with her mouth soft and her teal eyes full of him. He was definitely going to break, swim to her with quick strokes, and kiss her like she'd never been kissed.

She'd kissed him, every single time. It was *his* turn.

Instead of letting himself plunge down that sinkhole, he forced himself to ask, "Does your charity pay you a salary?" It was kind of a dumb question and really none of his business, but he needed her to talk and break this tension between them.

"I live off some of the sponsorship money that my social media creates but use most of it for my charity," she said, standing in chest deep water and swirling her hands through it. "When I first started, I was managing a preschool and daycare center."

"That's a good fit for you."

"I love children." Her face brightened and her eyes danced as she talked. Sadly for him, it made him fall even deeper for her. "I started my social media account, 'Love the Littles,' first to bring awareness to protecting children from domestic abuse, but then it grew into inspirational thoughts, quotes, and stories to help parents and caregivers. I gained so many followers that I started getting sponsor offers. Then my sponsors wanted me to offer giveaways of all kinds of products from diapers to online parenting classes and my followers grew, bringing even bigger sponsors."

"Wow, that's great. And you use your expertise and donations to help children and parents."

She nodded. "I try."

"You're remarkable, Tess."

Her full smile came out. "Thank you." She stared at him and said, "I love it when you say my name."

Whatever he was going to say got caught in his throat or disappeared from his brain. She loved it when he said her name. That was it. He was going to bury his guilt, push through this water, wrap her up tight, and kiss her until the helicopter came for them tomorrow.

Sadly, he didn't move. She gave him a watery smile and turned, pushing through the water and sliding into her flip flops. He followed her back to camp. They changed and got ready for bed. She excused herself to use the bathroom and he waited impatiently. It was their last night together. How was he going to tell her goodbye tomorrow, knowing he'd never see her again? He hated being all dramatic and fatalistic, but that was how he felt.

When she came back, he unzipped the tent and held it open for her. It wasn't that late, but there didn't seem to be much else to do but sleep. He considered telling her he was gifting her the half a million dollars Axel was supposed to pay him, but he knew she'd try to refuse. He'd talk to Axel about it tomorrow night. Brit didn't have much to look forward to in life besides working and trying to help others when he could. He might as well give the money to someone like Tess who would do great things with it.

As they lay down on their sleeping pads, a desperate ache was rising inside of him. Tomorrow. She'd be gone tomorrow. Would he be the worst person in the world if he held her tonight? He wouldn't kiss her, but just to hold her ... it would be a memory he could hold on to for a long time. He pleaded with the good Lord above for guidance and he didn't see a stop sign in front of his face. Was that his sign?

He edged a little closer and asked quietly, "Tess ... would you hate me if I asked you if I could hold you tonight?"

Tess let out the cutest little cry and said fervently, "I'd hate you if you didn't."

Brit pulled in a steadying breath. Words like that out of her beautiful mouth made him want to kiss her and never let her go. Instead of asking for a kiss, and hating himself for his weakness, he said gruffly, "Can you please roll away from me? If your face is right there ..." He swallowed hard and admitted, "I don't know how I'll stop myself from kissing you."

"Oh, Brit." Her voice wavered. "A big part of me wants to scream, 'To heck with your honor,' dive on top of you, and kiss you until you push me away."

Brit closed his eyes, trying to steel himself from that appealing image. "That's the problem," he admitted through a very dry throat. "I would *never* be able to push you away."

The only sound in the tent after his declaration was their ragged breathing. There was so much tension that he wanted to swipe his hand through the air and see if he could feel it. Tess said nothing, which made him irrationally sad. He missed her motor mouth, and it was his fault she'd lost her free-flowing tongue.

Tess slowly rolled onto her side, facing away from him, and scooted back until her back was against his chest. Brit fought to breathe as joy filled him. He wrapped one arm around her waist and threaded the other between her neck and the pillow. She sighed contentedly and put her hand over his.

"Thank you," he whispered.

"It's no hardship, believe me."

He smiled at that. Holding her close was definitely no hardship.

Tomorrow, when he had to say goodbye ... that would be hardship.

That would be like walking into a terrorist camp unarmed.

CHAPTER THIRTEEN

Tess didn't sleep much Friday night, but she didn't care. Brit's arms surrounding her all night long was a heaven she never thought she'd experience. If only she could think of a way around the promise he'd made to his deceased girlfriend, but she couldn't, and she loved him even deeper for staying true to that promise.

Horribly his honor meant they could never be together.

She'd always liked tragic romances: Romeo and Juliet, Kylo Ren and Rey, Heathcliff and Catherine, Allie and Noah—heck, she even liked Scarlett and Rhett, though she thought they were both selfish jerks.

Being in a tragic romance of her own was decidedly ... awful. Except for now, it wasn't too hard. She was still in Brit's arms and the sun hadn't risen yet.

Brit shifted behind her and his breath shortened.

"Are you awake?" she whispered.

"Yes," he whispered back.

"Why are we whispering?"

"I have no idea."

They both laughed, almost uneasily.

"It's like if we talk quietly real life won't come and wrench us apart," she said.

Brit nodded, tenderly brushing the hair from her neck. She trembled from his touch. His lips replaced his fingers and her neck warmed with a fire she wanted to feel every day of her life.

"Do you have any idea how beautiful you are?"

"No." She waited, hoping he'd tell her again. She'd never placed much stock in beauty, thinking her rounded shape wasn't that appealing. Her dimples made her cute and her eyes were a cool color, but her cheeks were definitely too chubby for her to be considered any kind of classic beauty.

His hand ran over her shoulder and down her arm, leaving tingles in its wake. "The most beautiful woman I've ever seen. Your hair, your eyes, your smooth skin, your lips."

Tess swallowed hard and admitted to him, "I've never seen myself as beautiful."

"You are. Believe me."

"I think you might just be prejudiced."

He chuckled and she felt it against her back. "Definitely. I am most definitely prejudiced to you, Tess." He rested his hand on her waist and rubbed along the curve of it. "You're even more beautiful to me because of how perfect you are on the inside."

"Thank you, Brit," she managed.

The tent was lightening as dawn approached.

"I guess we'd better get going," she said. "Find that stinking treasure."

"If that's what you want."

Tess thought that was an odd response. Yes, she wanted to

find the treasure and help more children and families, but all she really wanted was him, and she couldn't have him.

She stood quickly, unzipped the tent, and scurried out of it. She slid into her flip flops and hurried to look in their supplies at what was left for breakfast on their last morning. Their last morning together. She wanted to cry, but she bit her lip and blinked quickly. She couldn't be dissolving into tears all the time.

She looked over and Brit was standing just outside the tent. He looked incredible with his strong build, handsome face, and those dark eyes filled with concern for her.

"Tess ... are you all right?"

She straightened and flung a hand at him. "No, I am not all right. I come on this crazy adventure and we search over and over again for a treasure that's not even there, and that's not even the worst part of it."

He watched her cautiously as if she might implode.

"The worst part is I love every minute of being with you and I think I've fallen in love with you, but you're not free to love me back, ever."

His face tightened. He gave her that tortured look she'd glimpsed the first time they kissed.

"It's fine." She held up a hand. "I'm fine. I mean, not really, but what do you do, right? You've been dealing with this tragic promise you made for what ... ten, twelve years? I've only dealt with it for a day and a half and I can hardly handle it. I'm sorry. Let's just go search for the treasure. I don't need breakfast, do you?" Her stomach was far too upset to even think about food.

She grabbed her water bottle out of her backpack and hurried to the stream to fill it. She could feel him coming behind her. He wrapped his arms around her and pulled her back against him. Tess stayed there, allowing herself to rely on his strength.

Resting her hands on his arms, she closed her eyes and just let herself savor this moment with him close.

The sun rose and she didn't know how she'd leave this spot, but she said a prayer for strength and pulled from his arms. Turning to face him, she muttered, "I promise I'm much stronger than I'm acting."

He trailed his fingertips down her face. "You are incredibly strong. I'm so sorry I pulled you into this mess."

She looked him over and realized, even with how much it hurt, she wouldn't trade the love she felt for him. The pain was worth the falling in love, talking with him, laughing with him, the sweetness of their few shared kisses, and being in his arms last night. Next week when she was alone, she'd probably feel differently, but right now she wouldn't change anything. Except somehow miraculously erasing that promise to Kelley. But no, that was part of him, making him even more incredible and strong inside and out. Besides without that promise, he might already be married to some redhead named Tiffany. She loved him even more for loving redheads.

"Don't be sorry, Brit. I'll never regret this time with you."

He smiled sadly.

"You know what we're going to do?" she asked.

"No." He shook his head. "But I'm sure you'll tell me."

She nodded. "Yes, I will. We're going to forget about all this hard junk between us and have a good day. We'll search for treasure and talk and laugh and swim in our waterfall pool one more time and when that helicopter comes to get us this afternoon, we'll have had one of the best days of our lives."

Brit's smile broke through and she was stunned that this amazing man cared for her as deeply as he obviously did. "Thank you, Tess. I don't know anyone else who could equal your atti-tude. You really are *my* ray of sunshine."

Tess loved the inflection in his voice. She wished she'd dare suggest they forget his commitments and kiss the day away, but that wouldn't be fair to him or to Kelley. She felt a brief sting. Was Kelley watching them from heaven and hating Tess for trying to steal her man? But no, she didn't think it worked that way. If Kelley was watching, she would want Brit to be happy. But even if that was true, Tess wouldn't suggest that Brit forget his promise. She couldn't.

They covered most of the remaining area throughout the warm day. It was truly a tropical paradise here, but Tess's paradise was being with Brit. They talked and talked as the miles passed. Her ankle still ached, but she was walking well on it and she didn't tell Brit it hurt.

A little after noon, they found another bag with a clue.

Your treasure is right in front of you.

That flipped them both out for a while. They searched high and low, even trying to dig in the ground, but nothing.

As five o'clock approached and they knew their time was running out, Tess should've felt more disappointed they hadn't found the treasure, but she could only feel an impending doom knowing her time with Brit was at an end.

They returned to camp and she wondered if they could have one more swim in the waterfall pool, but they heard a helicopter approaching. She knew it wasn't Joe, but fear still made her blood run cold.

Brit's gaze darted to her. He took her hand and she immedi-ately felt settled and safe. They studied each other as the heli-copter landed up by the waterfall and then they heard the rotors cutting and voices approaching.

"You all right?" he asked.

She forced a smile she didn't feel. She wouldn't cause Brit any more agony. Turning from the pain in his dark eyes, she saw none other than Axel Dexter approaching, followed by a gorgeous, tall blonde woman and a cameraman. Tess held on to her smile.

"There they are," Axel called. "How was your week?" He grabbed Brit in a friendly hug but sobered a little bit as if he could feel the duress in the air. "Everything okay?"

Brit nodded quickly. "Tess was amazing. You heard what happened with Joe?"

Axel nodded, suddenly serious. He looked to Tess. "I am so sorry, Tess. I would never have put you in danger like that."

She acknowledged that with a nod and quickly changed the subject. "Wait until you see the pig attack and me falling down the waterfall."

Axel's eyes widened as the blonde gasped and pointed back at the waterfall. "You fell down that?"

"Well, close to it." She walked forward and extended her hand. "I'm Tess James. I haven't had the pleasure of meeting you yet."

"Emerald Taylor." She warmly shook her hand. "I'm a huge fan of yours, Tess. When Axel tasked me with finding the top charitable influencers on social media, you were my top pick from the beginning."

"Oh, thank you." Tess was amazed. This woman looked like she'd stepped off a magazine cover. Tess was dirty and probably smelly, but Emerald treated her like she was royalty.

"Now, the real question ..." Axel rubbed his hands together. "Did you each find your treasure?"

"No," Tess admitted, looking at Brit. She'd failed the children and she'd lost Brit. Well, that wasn't true; she'd never had him.

"No?" Axel's voice was all sad and droopy, like they'd killed his favorite pony or something.

"I thought only Tess was supposed to find a treasure?" Brit clarified.

Axel's brow wrinkled. "I thought ..." He looked back and forth between the two of them. "The clues? The clues didn't help?"

Tess frowned. For a brilliant billionaire, he was pretty daft. "No, they didn't help."

"Oh." Axel looked puzzled for a second, but then his face brightened. "You know what, Tess? I'm going to give you more time to figure out the clues and win that half a million dollars."

She blinked at him. More time with Brit? Were these beautiful people and the cameraman going to turn around and leave them here? Her heart raced with happiness as her gaze met Brit's. He had that tortured look in his eyes but also a brightness. Even though it would be hard to be together longer, knowing it could never last, neither of them would turn down any chance for stolen minutes.

"Well, let's go." Axel interrupted their silent exchange. "Leave everything here. A crew is on their way to clean it up."

"But I thought you said—" Tess was very confused. "How can I have more time to figure out the clues if I'm not here where the treasure is?"

Axel's eyes twinkled again. "I'll give you some time. I know you'll figure it out." He turned and escorted Emerald back up to the helicopter.

Brit waited and Tess walked in front of him. She turned back to look at him and said, "Is your friend all there ... mentally?"

Brit chuckled and gestured to the cameraman still videoing. "Most of the time."

"Hmm."

She kept walking. What was Axel trying to tell her? How could she win the money?

But most importantly, how could she say goodbye to Brit tonight?

CHAPTER FOURTEEN

The helicopter flight, the testimonies at the police station, and even the flight back home passed surprisingly quickly. Tess cleaned up, happy to take a shower in the airplane bathroom. Emerald had clean clothes for her and Brit and some hair products and nice-smelling lotion and lip gloss for her.

They all ate dinner together on the flight back, takeout from a Thai truck on Kauai that Axel raved about. It was delicious. Tess enjoyed watching Brit and Axel interact and reminisce and Emerald was impressive and fun to talk to, plying her with questions about her charity and her plans. Her mind should be going crazy trying to figure out what the treasure was since the clock was ticking, but Brit was the only thing on her mind.

Though the camera guy videoed everything, and there was an undeniable mixture of tension and regret arcing between her and Brit, Tess enjoyed the time. She tried to catalogue everything about Brit in her mind, the way he kept sneaking glances at her, his tender yet hesitant smile when their eyes met, the laughs that Axel cajoled out of him. She doubted very much that her tough military hero was on social media, so these might be her last glimpses of him.

Tess glanced at the cameraman. Eventually, their portion of the show would air, so she'd at least have that. What parts would they use? Would they show their romance at all? She hadn't had the GoPro on for any of their kisses, but the camp cameras probably picked some of them up. There was still plenty that the producers could pull out to create the heartbreaking romance between them. Nobody but her and Brit would ever know why they couldn't be together. She could already imagine her social media followers, and worse her mom and friends, hounding her about it.

They descended into the exclusive private airport east of Phoenix where she'd left her car. It was almost eleven and she should be tired, but she was wide awake thinking about how this goodbye would go. The pilot landed smoothly and they all stretched and exited the plane. The rest of them were flying on to Texas tonight. It was nice of them to walk her out, but she only wanted a private goodbye with Brit.

It was still warm in the dry Arizona air. She instantly missed her tropical paradise with Brit. Even if it had been a tent with premade meals and her only bath a waterfall pool, it had been a week she'd never forget.

Emerald gave her a quick hug. "It was lovely to meet you. Thank you for inspiring me."

Tess grinned at the beautiful woman, wondering why Axel wasn't dating her, but she didn't sense any sparks between the two of them. "You're lovely," Tess said. "It was fabulous to meet you."

Emerald smiled beautifully. Tess was going to have to Google her. She'd bet she was a supermodel.

Axel shook her hand. "Thanks for doing the show, Tess. I can hardly wait to watch all the footage you recorded." He winked at her, as if knowing she'd turned the camera off at times. She hadn't done it on purpose, but it hadn't been her first priority.

Tess looked to the man who she wanted to be her first priority. He studied her with an unreadable expression in his dark eyes.

Axel looked back and forth between them and said with a sneaky smile, "You call me tomorrow when you figure out what the treasure is and I'll transfer that money."

She stared at him. Maybe she could get some clues from him right now. Some real clues. "So the treasure wasn't buried or hidden in a tree?"

"Nope." He patted her arm like she was a small child. "You'll figure it out. You're a brilliant lady." With that, he turned and escorted Emerald back to the airplane. Emerald gave one last wave before they disappeared. Unfortunately, the camera guy stayed.

Brit was focused on her, but his eyes flickered to the camera. "I'm going to walk Miss James to her car," he said very formally and firmly.

The guy gave an imperceptible nod. With the airport all lit up, her car was visible from here, but walking to her car would give them some privacy. She had her purse and phone back, but she hadn't looked at either. She swung her purse over her shoulder and walked away. Brit fell into step beside her. Neither of them said anything. What was there to say? She should be plying him for ideas on what the treasure could be, but all she could think about was that she'd never see him again. She could find other ways to raise money for her charity, but she'd never find another man to replace Brit.

They reached her car. She unlocked it, opened the door, dropped her purse inside, and then turned to face him. What she wouldn't give for him to pin her against the car and kiss her, but one look in his eyes and she knew it wouldn't happen. Dang his honor. No matter how sad it made her she loved him for his honor too.

She smiled tremulously up at him, willing herself not to cry. She had over an hour drive home and she could listen to Adele and cry the entire way for all anybody knew.

"Thanks," she murmured, staring into his dark eyes. "That's so insufficient for how I feel and everything you've done for me, but ..." Her voice broke and she looked away. "That's all I've got."

"You've been incredible, Tess," he said in a low, gravelly voice. "I don't know anyone who would have dealt with ... everything, as well as you did."

She nodded her thanks. It seemed that was all he had too. She looked up at him. He brushed his knuckles across her jaw, gave her a sad smile, and then turned and walked away. Tess felt like she was being torn apart. She couldn't do it. She couldn't just let him walk away without knowing.

"Brit," his name ripped from her.

He turned back.

She took a tentative step toward him. "I admire your strength, physically, and your strength of character."

"Thank you," he said, his brow squiggled as if not sure what she was getting at, why she was extending the torture of this goodbye to tell him she admired him.

"Though I respect the promise you made to Kelley ... I never promised not to fall in love with you."

His eyes widened, but he took a tentative step forward and admitted, "No matter how hard I fought it ... I've fallen in love with you too, Tess."

That was it. All her resolve to stay strong broke. She ran at him, throwing herself against him. He caught her, swinging her slightly but settling and holding her fiercely against him. They both knew it would be the last time they'd touch.

Tess looked up at him and said, "And I never promised I wouldn't kiss you again."

Brit's eyes widened and then filled with desire.

Tess arched onto tiptoes, pulled his head down to hers, and kissed him. She kissed him with all the love and anguish rolling around inside of her. She loved and hated this kiss. It was so full of desperation and need. She never, ever wanted it to end, but even as Brit kissed her back and his kiss conveyed how badly he hated to say goodbye, she knew it was time. Time for goodbye.

She yanked herself from his arms, tried to swallow down the sob that rose, then turned and ran for her car. Wrenching the door open, she slid inside and slammed the door. She fumbled for her keys and eventually shoved them into the ignition and started the car.

The lights flashed onto Brit, who still hadn't moved. He blinked against the brightness but stayed right there, as if he couldn't be the one who walked away. With a heaving sob, Tess jammed the car into reverse, spun out of the parking spot, and floored it out of there. One last look in her rearview confirmed it. He still hadn't moved.

Tess didn't even need music. Tears streaked continually down her face without any help from Adele at all.

CHAPTER FIFTEEN

Brit watched Tess race out of the parking lot. His chest was tight and his entire body hurt as if he had the flu. Her leaving was worse than he could've imagined. His stomach turned as he watched her drive away much too quickly. Then irrational fear filled him. What if she got in a wreck? He wanted to chase after her and beg her to slow down. Should he call her and warn her? Why had he let her drive away? He realized he didn't even have her number. Then he also realized calling her could distract her and put her in even more danger.

Dropping his head, he said a fervent prayer for her to make it home safe. Sick but not sure what else he could do, he turned and trudged back to the plane.

Axel was beaming at him and Emerald's face was full of expectation as well. The cameraman had finally set his camera down and was looking through the footage Tess had taken on the GoPro.

"So ... what are your future plans?" Axel asked excitedly.

The pilot shut the door and headed for the cockpit. Brit dropped wearily into a leather chair. "No future plans."

"What?" Axel was so expressive. That one word was as if Brit had told him he'd disbanded the military.

The plane started taxiing to the runway, but Axel leapt to his feet and started pacing in front of Brit's chair. "What do you mean, no future plans? You two are perfect for each other."

Brit heaved out a breath and did up his seatbelt. "Sit down for takeoff, Axel."

His friend glared at him, and unfortunately buckled in right next to him. He lowered his voice. "I'm not supposed to admit this, but I set up this entire thing for you and Tess to meet."

Brit's head felt like it got whiplash he spun so quickly to stare at his friend. "Are you serious?"

"Yeah." He was almost talking in a whisper now, but the cameraman was back a little ways and one look at Emerald revealed she knew exactly what Axel was saying and didn't approve of him sharing it. "When I first inherited the money, I tried to give it away. There's too much money and it keeps on coming with all the investments and property and the oil. I set up my mom and some of the people in my old neighborhood paying off their houses and giving them monthly annuities. Then I gave a million dollars to each of the men I served with."

Brit's heart was ripped out and driving away with Tess, but he found himself intrigued by what Axel was sharing.

"Some of them changed their lives with it for the better, but some didn't. Kind of like when someone wins the lottery and is worse off." He shrugged, though his blue eyes looked sad. "Some of them were actually in a much worse spot for being gifted the money and that made me feel awful. So I decided to try a different approach this time. I wanted to see if the men and women I gave the money to worked for it, in a sense, if they would manage and appreciate it better." He cleared his throat and continued, "As I started brainstorming I couldn't get you out of my mind. How much I'd always liked and admired you. How you lost Kelley."

Brit's chest tightened. His friend didn't know the half of it.

"So I looked into your men that were out of active duty and had Emerald research each of you and find the right women for a match."

"What is this? Some big matchmaking game for you?" Brit grunted, suddenly angry. Axel had no right to set him up then rip his heart apart like this. But he couldn't regret the time with Tess, no matter how it had to end.

"No. I mean, that might add a fun element to some of the couples and the weeks, but it was only you that I really wanted to find the perfect person for. Tess is perfect for you, isn't she?"

"Yes," he admitted. The plane soared east toward Texas, but he'd left his heart in Arizona.

"Then why aren't there future plans?"

Brit closed his eyes and pressed his head back against the leather seat. He didn't even know what to tell Axel. He certainly wasn't sharing his vow to Kelley with him. Only Tess was privileged to that secret.

"Come on, man." Axel jostled his arm as if this was some game. "I set you up perfectly. Tess is incredible and you were all alone. Then all the clues, the treasure. You had to see it."

Brit opened his eyes and glared at Axel. "There was no stinking treasure. Why did you set her up like that?"

Axel spread his hands. "Tess will get the answer to what her treasure is soon, and her money. You see the answer, right?"

Brit was so tired. He hadn't slept at all last night while

holding Tess. She was the treasure for him. "Tess was the only treasure on that island."

Axel grinned and punched his fists in the air. "Yes! You got it. I knew you'd figure it out."

Brit grunted. Tess was the best treasure he could imagine, but she wasn't his, no matter how much he wanted her to be. He changed the subject before he stupidly told the entire story to Axel. "Are all my men going to be searching for a treasure with hidden meanings?"

"Nah. Every week is going to be completely different. Some have to get from point A to point B, some just have to survive. They'll be all over the globe, in all kinds of situations. It's going to be fun. I've even recruited your beautiful sister to do a special weeklong rafting trip."

Brit stared at him. It didn't surprise him that Axel was calling Kinsley beautiful. She was, but Axel was also lauded to be quite the ladies' man. "Who will Kinsley be with?"

"She won't be with anyone. She'll be the guide." He looked a little possessive of her, and Brit's eyes widened. "She's amazing, that sister of yours."

Brit nodded in agreement and rubbed at the growth on his jaw. He'd showered in the airplane bathroom but he was ready for a shave. "Just make sure she stays safe."

Axel nodded seriously but said, "I think Kinsley is pretty adept at taking care of herself."

Brit knew that was true, but she was still his little sister. He wondered what contact Axel and Kinsley had had. She was a few years younger than them and Brit hadn't known they were friends.

"I'm really excited about each of them." He slanted a look at Brit. "But I was most excited for you and Tess. You fell hard for her, right?" He grinned and leaned in as if Brit would share all the details.

"It doesn't matter," Brit said miserably. "It isn't going to work out."

"What?" Axel protested. "Why not?"

Brit gave him a look that would've had his men running for cover.

Axel simply raised his eyebrows and demanded, "Why not?"

"It's none of your business."

Axel looked like a little boy who'd been denied a cookie.

"I'm going to take a nap now. Oh, and Axel, donate my half a million dollars to Tess's charity."

Axel's eyes widened and his smile grew.

Brit closed his eyes and turned his head away. He didn't want to talk to Axel right now or have him pull out the truth of how he'd fallen for Tess. He wanted to simply remember her, catalog each conversation, look, and touch in his brain so he didn't lose the memories too quickly.

It was going to be a lonely stretch of life without her.

CHAPTER SIXTEEN

Tess somehow made it through the next couple of days. When her parents, neighbors, or friends asked about her week, she told them all the good parts. She kept the great parts, meaning every tender interaction with Brit, to herself. She stayed positive and worked hard and stewed about what Axel thought she should know about the treasure.

Her phone rang and she almost didn't answer it, an unknown local number. "Hello?" she asked cautiously.

"Miss James. This is Norene Vilmar from Golden Credit Union."

Her bank? She wasn't rolling in money, but she had plenty in her account to cover everything. Right? It was a sting not to get the money, but she'd be fine. She'd work hard and still help a lot of families. "Oh, yes. What can I help you with?"

"We wanted to get your approval on the half-million dollar deposit from Mr. Dexter. Also, we'd be happy to offer a financial advisor to help with distributing the funds and tax planning."

"Um ..." Tess had no response. "What?"

What was Axel playing at? She hadn't won the treasure.

"Yes, Miss James." She waited then. "Miss James?"

"Sorry ... Can I call you back?"

"Certainly." She rattled off her direct number. "Please call at your earliest convenience."

"Thank you," she mumbled, hanging up the phone. Sinking into her couch, she stared at the phone in a stupor. She hadn't found the treasure. What was Axel doing? A happy surge went through her. A half-million dollars? Sheesh! With that much money, she could help so many children and families in America and in third-world countries.

She felt excitement and nerves as she found Axel's number in her cell phone and pushed on it.

"Tess!" he greeted her happily. "I wondered when you'd be calling me. You figured out what the treasure was."

Tess looked out her window at the pine trees that gave her town their name. "Um, no. I called to thank you for the half-million-dollar deposit." She suddenly grew uncertain. "That is, if you meant to deposit it?"

"Of course I did." His voice was loud and excited. "But that money was from Brit."

"Excuse me?" She clung to the phone, feeling dizzy.

"Yeah." Axel's voice softened. "He insisted that I give you the money he was supposed to earn, for your charity."

"Wow," she managed. "I don't know what to say."

"Maybe you could call and thank him," Axel suggested.

Her breath whooshed out. Could she? She wanted to thank him with much more than a phone call, but she didn't want to make their separation any harder on him.

"Did you figure out what the treasure is?" Axel asked. "I'd really like to give you more money."

Tess was only focused on Brit. How could he be so generous? He deserved that money, but he'd given it to her, to the children. "I don't know what the treasure is," she admitted.

"Come on, Tess. You're brilliant. You got this."

She shook her head, in awe at Brit's gift. "No, but I'm so grateful for Brit. Thank you for making it possible for me to meet him."

If only they could be together.

"Of course. I'm sorry you didn't get the treasure."

"It's okay. I really appreciate the adventure and opportunity and getting to know Brit."

"Why aren't you together?" Axel suddenly demanded. "You have to admit you're perfect for each other. Brit's been through so much, but he's the best guy. Emerald and I both think you're going to make him so happy."

Tess thought they were perfect for each other too, but it wasn't to be. Axel had no clue about Brit's promise, and it wasn't her place to tell him. "Axel ... it's not my place to explain, but Brit and I can't be together."

"Please, Tess, give him a chance. A lot of guys struggle after being in the military, especially Special Ops, and he has the extra hit of losing ... Did he tell you?"

"He told me about Kelley." Axel didn't know the half of it.

"So, yeah, that was hard, but he's strong. I promise he would treat you like a princess and it's obvious how much he loves you."

Tess would've laughed at the ludicrousness of her having this conversation with billionaire heartthrob Axel Dexter, but she was too messed up emotionally over Brit. She gulped, feeling the tears coming. "Axel, thank you so much for everything. I'm so sorry things didn't turn out with Brit and I." A sob choked her. "Goodbye."

She hung up the phone.

Turning the ringer off, she simply sat there. Half a million dollars. It was insane. She'd do so much good with that money. If only she could feel happier about it. She couldn't see much happiness in the future without Brit. More tears and body-shaking sobs overtook her.

CHAPTER SEVENTEEN

B rit went home to Cedar Hills, Texas and his condo not far from his parents' house. He needed to figure out what to do with his life now. It stretched empty and lonely before him. After stopping in to see his parents, he went to church with them and then stayed after to meet with his pastor from childhood on up. Pastor Butler was a great guy and Brit found himself telling him ... everything.

Apparently, since he'd shared the secret with Tess, it was easier to let it slip out a second time. His pastor listened but didn't give him any sage advice. He was impressed with Brit's sense of honor and integrity but hated to have him be alone his entire life, especially when he'd met someone like Tess who Pastor Butler agreed sounded incredible.

Brit went home feeling a little better after sharing the burden, but it was depressing that not even that inspired man had any advice for him. He spent the next few days applying for security jobs. It seemed an okay fit for him, nothing too exciting, but he couldn't get himself too excited about anything, not without Tess. He missed her like a constant ache. Would it get easier? It had to or he wouldn't survive.

He prayed hard for help and inspiration. Nothing came.

Wednesday morning, he got a call from the church's secretary asking him to meet with Pastor Butler that night. He quickly agreed, hoping and praying this might be the answer he was waiting for. Something had to change and soon. A future of working security and never loving Tess? He couldn't do it.

After the eight weeks of not contacting his buddies was over he'd get a hold of Tanner and Tagg and find the most aggressive anti-trafficking crew they'd ever worked with. He'd join forces with his friends who risked their lives every day fighting the traffickers from the inside out. He'd hope and pray he could give his life for a cause like that.

Even the thought of leaving Tess here on earth ripped him apart. He loved her more than he could even put a description on. His feelings for Kelley had been real but immature. He'd been too selfish and undeveloped emotionally to know what love was. He knew now. Love to him was Tess.

He hurried into the church at the appointed time and to the pastor's office. When he rapped on the slightly open door, Pastor Butler called, "Come in."

Pushing the door open, he strode in and froze. A beautiful, dark-haired young woman sat on one of the hard chairs in front of the pastor's desk. Her head was turned partially away from him, but that profile was hauntingly familiar.

"Kelley?" he rasped.

Had Kelley's angel come to tell him how to proceed? That was insane, right? But if anybody could invite an angel for a visit it would probably be Pastor Butler.

She turned and glared at him.

Not Kelley. His mind whirred and it clicked. "Marley?"

The young woman nodded tersely. He'd always liked Kelley's little sister. She'd come on dates with them sometimes and always stayed close to them when they were at Kelley's house.

"It's been a long time. How are you doing?" His mind was quickly filling in the details. His mom had told him how Marley got mixed up with the wrong crowd, got into drugs, and ran away from home after Kelley died. Marley had been with Kelley in the accident. He couldn't imagine how hard it had been on her. She looked good, and healthy, except for the scowl on her face.

"I'm okay." She looked to Pastor Butler. "Can we get this over with?"

The older man nodded. "Of course. Please tell Britton. Whatever you feel you should tell him."

Marley studied the portrait of the Savior behind the desk, avoiding both of their gazes as she started talking. "I used to really like you, when you and Kelley were dating. You were always nice to include me and pay for me and stuff. But then I got jealous because you seemed to be all she cared about."

"I'm sorry," Britton said lamely. It had been almost twelve years. Marley had only been thirteen or fourteen when Kelley died. Surely she was over feeling jealous of time Kelley spent with him. The crusty look she gave him said maybe she wasn't.

"When we got in the wreck," she sniffed and Britton felt his body tense, "she was a mess, blood streaming down her face, and her body was so beat up ..." She broke off and twisted her hands together before continuing quietly, "I knew she couldn't survive, but I couldn't stand the thought of it. She was my hero, my best friend ..." She swallowed hard. "She kept saying something. She repeated it over and over again before she died."

Brit held his breath. It had to be about him or why would she have brought him here? He waited anxiously, but she didn't say anything for at least a twenty count.

Finally, she started talking again. "The message was for you. She begged me to tell you ..." She took a deep breath and said in a monotone voice, as if she'd heard these words over and over again, "'Tell Brit I release him from his vow. Tell him I want him to move on and find love.'"

Brit felt like somebody had shoved a burning knife through his chest. He stared at Marley, wondering if she was going to take it back.

He looked to Pastor Butler, who nodded. "When we talked on Sunday, I wondered if Marley would have any insight for you, since she was there when Kelley passed and I knew it was the reason she's ... struggled for so long. I had no idea she had this much insight. How do you feel, son?"

He felt shocked and excited and very confused. He looked to Marley, who had lost her belligerence and was twisting her hands in her lap.

"Why didn't you tell me before now?" His voice was shaky. He was pretty certain she never would've told him if the pastor hadn't intervened.

She shrugged and wouldn't look at him. "I was a thirteen-year-old girl devastated by seeing my sister die. Even as she was dying, all she cared about was *you*." Her voice rose. "I lost my sister and what did you do? Did you even mourn her? No, you didn't even come for the funeral. Then you go on to be some Navy SEAL Captain hero who everybody in Cedar Hills is so proud of. While a part of me died and I lived for my next hit and didn't know how I'd keep breathing." The spite in her voice dug at him.

"Mourn her?" he asked. "I couldn't get leave for her funeral, but I've mourned her nonstop. I haven't let myself date or fall in love for twelve years because of my promise to Kelley."

That wasn't technically true. He'd fallen in love with Tess.

Tess! Even though he was frustrated that Marley hadn't told him before now, he could understand that she'd been young, jealous of his relationship with her sister, and then gotten into drugs. In her mind, him not quitting the military and coming home to mourn showed he didn't care.

Pushing all of that away, a joy rose in him that had him almost as choked up as the anger of a moment before had. "I'm sorry, Marley. I can't imagine how hard this has been on you."

She lifted her eyebrows as if he had no idea.

"Can you please tell me exactly what Kelley said again?"

She sighed and said, "'Tell Brit I release him from his vow. Tell him I want him to move on and find love.'" She repeated the words woodenly, but with exactly the same phrasing she'd used earlier. It was obvious those words had played through her mind often the past twelve years.

Brit wanted to sprint all the way to Arizona. Kelley had released him from his vow. She wanted him to move on and find love. He could be happy. Twelve long years of feeling bound to a promise that he had been too immature and short-sighted to make in the first place, but he'd stuck by it because he'd made it. Now he felt ... free ... and so in love with Tess.

He stood and walked to Marley. Sticking out his hand, he waited. She stood and shook it. He pulled her in and gave her a hug. She gasped and didn't return the hug, but she didn't punch him either.

"Thank you, Marley. Thank you for telling me. I know it was hard for you. I'm so sorry about Kelley. I hope you can also move on and find love and happiness and peace."

He pulled back. Marley was crying. "Thank you, Brit. I forgive you for stealing my sister from me." She smiled through her tears.

He smiled too.

He moved to Pastor Butler and shook his hand. "Thank you. Thank you for everything."

Pastor Butler patted his shoulder. "Of course. It's what I do. Bringing happiness and peace to the world." He winked. "I think you need to go."

"Yes, sir, I do." Brit hurried from the room, yanking his phone out and booking a flight into Flagstaff. He could only pray it wouldn't take too long.

He had to get to Tess.

CHAPTER EIGHTEEN

Tess was recording a video for all of her social media sites in her backyard, with the pine trees as background. It was a fun video, telling her followers about the insane gift from Axel Dexter—Axel had texted that Brit didn't want his name mentioned—and all the ways she was going to expand to help more children. It hurt that Brit didn't want her to even thank him, but she knew he was just being humble. She'd wanted to call him but didn't know if it would torture both of them with what they couldn't have. She'd mailed off a thank you card instead. So lame, but it was all she could handle without running to Texas and throwing herself at him.

She heard crunching on the gravel drive out front. Finishing the video, she dropped her phone in her back pocket and walked around to see who was coming to visit. A silver car that she didn't recognize pulled into the driveway. She squinted to see through the sun's glare on the windshield but could only tell it was a dark-haired man.

The door sprung open and Brit stepped out.

She fell back a step and put her hand over her mouth. "Brit?"

He looked incredible, tall, strong, handsome, dressed in a short-sleeved button down shirt and navy slacks. "Tess." He said her name so beautifully, so joyfully, and took a step toward her.

"Thank you for the insane donation," she said.

"Oh." He lifted his hands. "The children need the money more than I do."

She smiled. Why had he come? It was incredible to see him, but nothing could've changed. Would they have to go through the torture of saying goodbye all over again?

Brit walked across the driveway, stopping in front of her. "Tess." He looked so happy, so at peace. His dark eyes sparkled at her. There was none of the torture in his gaze. It was clear and he looked free. "Something incredible happened."

Her heart started beating quicker. Had Kelley come to see him as an angel and released him from his vow? He reached out his hands, as if he couldn't stand to not touch her. She put both of her palms against his and felt the rightness of his touch.

"I've missed you," she rushed out.

He chuckled. "Not nearly as bad as I've missed you. There's so much to tell you, but there's something I need to do first ..."

He tugged her closer, wrapped his arms around her, and kissed her. The kiss was warm and strong and full of love and devotion. This was no goodbye kiss. This was all about hello, and many future hellos.

He pulled back and she knew her hair was disheveled and her lips were all plump, and all she wanted to do was kiss him again. "You kissed me," she said in awe.

He chuckled. "It's about time, right?"

"Dang straight." She laughed and she almost kissed him

again, but she had to know. "What happened, Brit? You're so ... free."

"I am free." He held her close, staring down at her with a happy grin. "Kelley's sister, Marley. She was with Kelley in the accident. Kelley told her before she died that she released me from my vow. She wanted me to find love and happiness and live my life. Apparently, she said it over and over again before she died." He lost his smile, growing serious as he told her the sad details of the accident and Marley's animosity.

Tess hugged him tight. She was grateful he'd learned about this, but she was sure even twelve years later, it hurt to hear the details of his girlfriend's death. Finally, she felt it wouldn't be disrespectful to ask, "Why did Marley wait so long to tell you?"

"She was thirteen when the accident happened. She resented me and when I didn't come home for the funeral, she thought I didn't care. She didn't understand that I was deployed in Afghanistan and couldn't come home. She also got into drugs and ran away from home. She's been quite a mess but is trying to get her life right now."

"Wow. I'm so sorry for Marley, and Kelley."

"Thank you."

He simply held her for a few wonderful minutes, then gazed down at her with a twinkle in his eye. "So I'm looking at relocating to Pine, Arizona. Do you know of any job openings?"

She stared at him in wonder. "Do you have any security experience?"

"As a matter of fact, I do."

"Well, I might be hiring. You see, some incredible man who wants to remain anonymous and his crazy generous billionaire friend gave me an insane amount of money. I'll be traveling to some third-world countries, potentially dangerous situations, to set up charitable donations and educational opportunities for local children and families."

"Sounds like you will need an experienced security professional and maybe somebody who's traveled extensively." He raised his eyebrows. "Anything else in the job description?"

"Hmm." She tilted her head to the side and then grinned shyly. "This security expert better also be an expert kisser."

"Oh. Hmm. I might be in trouble there. I haven't had a lot of hands-on experience the past twelve years. It seems women have to keep kissing me first."

She grinned. "I think I can help you with the hands-on experience. And I don't mind kissing you first."

His dark eyes glinted dangerously at her as he said, "Well, I mind. You've had your chance to kiss me first. It's my turn."

Tess's grin faded as he pulled her close and proceeded to kiss her.

She wouldn't complain at all about him taking his turn.

———

I hope you loved this start to the new Survive the Romance series. Keep reading for an excerpt of: *Romancing the Escape*. Find the first three books here. More to come soon!

Romancing the Treasure
Romancing the Escape
Romancing the Boat

ROMANCING THE ESCAPE

Rania's pulse had sped up at the sound of Tanner's laughter and the sight of his grin. Wow. She'd recognized that he was handsome and his face had been crafted by the good Lord's most accomplished angels, but seeing him with a genuine grin, not a smirky, condescending look like before, took him to Thor status in her mind. She found herself wanting to yank more grins out of that macho, military persona.

The thrum of a helicopter approaching pulled her attention away, thankfully before she said or did anything she'd regret. They both paused and watched as the helicopter swooped in a few minutes later. It landed behind the house and out of sight.

"Should we?" Tanner reached out as he had earlier when they'd gotten into their tease about him being a gentleman and she thought he might touch her, but he stopped himself and gestured again.

"Sure." She marched along the dock and onto a cleared path that led to the house. Tanner fell into step beside her and she was hyperaware of him. When his arm brushed hers she felt her pulse race again. What was she doing letting herself react to him? She had dated a large variety of men and wasn't interested in settling down anytime soon, especially with a jerk, woman-hater who was a too-stiff military type.

A man bounded around the side of the house, grinned, and threw his hands wide when he saw them. "Hello you beautiful people."

Axel Dexter's amazing assistant, Emerald Taylor had first contacted Rania about the show and told her she'd have the chance to meet the famous billionaire, America's most eligible bachelor currently, but she hadn't known when to expect him. He was an extremely handsome man with his blond hair and polished face. He was wearing a Brioni suit that didn't fit in this jungle atmosphere. Maybe if the house had been restored it could be a place for an Axel house party.

She felt Tanner's gaze and glanced at him. He was staring at her as if assessing her reaction to Axel. She tilted her chin and ignored him.

"Hello!" she called back. "Fancy meeting you here."

Axel chuckled and jogged across the path until he was in front of them. He reached his hand out to her first. "Rania Williams. You are a light and an inspiration. Thank you for gracing us with your presence."

He had too smooth of a tongue for Rania but her impression of him had always been a nice friendly guy and being face to face with him only increased that perception. "Thank you for gracing my charity with half a million dollars."

He threw back his head and laughed. "You have to earn it first, pretty lady."

Tanner stiffened at her side at the compliment.

Axel released her hand, turned to Tanner, and grabbed him in a manly backslapping hug. Tanner was obviously surprised and only feebly reciprocated. "Tanner McKay." Axel pulled back, resting his hands on Tanner's shoulders. "Sorry you don't even know me but I feel like we should be the best of friends. I've spoken at length with Brit about you and all he had was praise for you."

Rania's eyebrows involuntarily raised and Tanner noticed and gave her an embarrassed half smile. Axel was naturally profuse but this was still high praise. Maybe her military guy wouldn't be a class-one jerk.

"Thank you, sir," Tanner said, gracious but stiff.

"None of this sir garbage. We're like brothers, you and I." Axel grinned broadly but then sobered. "I honor your service to our country in the military and as you continue to give your life fighting the trafficking battle. Thank you, my friend."

Tanner nodded, relaxing a little bit. "Thank you."

Axel released Tanner's shoulders and turned to include Rania as well. "Thank you both. You are fighting a battle that in my mind is one of the most important causes of our day. My prayers are with you and hopefully soon my money will be as well." His grin returned as he rubbed his hands together. "Now to your challenge for the week."

Rania's stomach erupted in butterflies. Would they have to swim in the ocean for six days evading sharks and surviving on the fish Tanner could spear? Were there poisonous snakes crawling all over the island and they'd have to avoid them?

Axel turned and gestured toward the large mansion, walking that direction. "I purchased this island last month. I plan on renovating the entire home and making it a private retreat for church groups, employees, and friends, but first I'm going to let you two have some *fun* here."

They walked on a semi-cleared path toward the wraparound front porch. As they got closer Rania felt an almost sinister feeling wash over her. Awful things had happened in this home and she suddenly wanted to run back to Axel's bright, shiny yacht and sail far away from here. All the shutters were screwed shut with heavy bolts and a stack of heavy wood planks rested by the front door. She wondered if there was any natural light in there.

They walked up the thick wooden stairs which squeaked in protest and onto the wide front porch. It wasn't too run down but she understood why Axel wanted to renovate it to cleanse the dark feeling here. If she owned it she'd probably burn it to the ground and start over.

"As Emerald and I discussed how to bring awareness to the trafficking battle this week, I knew this house was the perfect solution." He paused next to the nine-foot front door. "You see for over three hundred years this place has been used by everything from rum runners to drug runners and also as a prison and exchange spot for slavery."

Tanner stiffened beside her. "I've heard of this place," he said quietly.

Axel nodded to him. "When the French External Security elite team did a raid here and found the entire basement filled with drugs, the property reverted to the French government. They auctioned it off and I bought it. This place will never be used for drugs or trafficking again and once I renovate it and have my priest bless it, the stain of the past won't be forgotten but thankfully won't be felt any longer. But first, you two have your challenge here."

Rania was getting increasingly uncomfortable and felt her stomach roll. She swallowed to keep from throwing up. Could she stay on this property where so many people had been imprisoned? That would be challenge enough for the week.

Axel threw the door wide, pulled out his phone, and switched on the flashlight. He beamed it around until he found a light switch and then flipped it on. The light from above illuminated a wide open hallway with an office-type space to the right and what was probably a sitting room to the left. Both were devoid of furniture besides built-in bookshelves and fireplaces. Everything was clean. It was actually in decent condition and though the windows were all covered with shutters it was bright and would've been semi-welcoming without the ghosts of the past haunting it.

"My people have come in and scoured the place but there's still an ominous feeling here."

Rania nodded her agreement. Too ominous. Hopefully he didn't expect them to stay in this house. Even if it did have power and running water, she would prefer camping on the beach for a week. It was much hotter in the house than outside with no ocean breeze to give fresh air. It felt stale and awful.

"So, to your challenge." He walked briskly through the wide hallway. They followed. Past a large kitchen he pulled open a door with stairs leading down. The uneasiness tripled at the sight of those dark stairs and trepidation about the unknown made her head pound. "Careful walking down here," he cautioned.

There was no light down here. He held his phone light and started the descent. Tanner's face was taut as he gestured her to go first. Rania clung to the railing and Axel shone the light back so she wasn't in the dark. She slowly descended the steep stairs, feeling the change in temperature from the sultry warmth of the Caribbean to a chilly basement. She hit level concrete and edged out of the way so Tanner and the cameraman could come down.

There was an odd mix of bleach and mold down here. It made her want to cover her nose. Tanner gave her an encouraging look as he reached the concrete landing next to her. She really wanted to sprint out of here but as the cameraman descended she remembered why she was here. Half a million to help protect and rescue children. She could do this. Oh man she hoped she could do this. Squeezing her eyes shut she said a prayer, simply, "Please help me."

She felt a hand cover hers and startled as she realized Tanner was not only touching her but comforting her. He leaned in. "Are you all right?"

She shrugged, not sure how to respond. She was definitely not all right but what choice did she have but to see this through. She really appreciated his support. At least she'd have a tough, brave military hero with her. Being alone down here would've had her huddled in a corner bawling.

Axel kept moving so they slowly followed him. The ceiling was tall enough that Axel and Tanner didn't have to duck, but just barely. Axel walked through the opening, a sliding barred door and into a prison. An actual prison with steel bars and everything. His bobbing phone flashlight made the shadows and the light glinting off those bars seem even more terrifying.

Oh, no. Rania's stomach turned over and she had to swallow several times to keep the nausea from manifesting itself. Tanner's hand around hers was the only thing that kept her from puking or blacking out. Suddenly instead of facing this alone she felt like she was facing it as part of a couple. That was crazy though. She and Tanner weren't a couple and after Brian's betrayal she didn't much want to find her other half.

Axel stopped walking and flipped on a bright camp light that was set on top of a table. The light thankfully illuminated the space. Rania clung to Tanner's hand as they walked into the prison. Simply being inside those bars, even with the gate open, made her want to run.

Instead she forced herself to look around, cataloging everything in an attempt to not focus on where they were. She fought hard to push away the evil, sadness, and death that seemed to be pressing in on her. There was the table and a couple of chairs. Piled on the table were the camp light, stacks of premade meals, water bottles, and other supplies. In the far right corner there was a toilet and sink with a curtain. In the far left there were two sleeping pads with blankets and pillows. If she had to guess, the room was probably about twenty by forty.

"So ..." Axel stopped and gestured around. "I apologize that it is a bit morbid but nobody said these challenges were going to be a walk in the park."

They both nodded. They'd signed their lives away, including injury and death to be part of the show and the challenge to win the money. She was very grateful that Tanner still held on to her hand. She didn't know him and didn't know if he'd thrust her away as soon as Axel and the cameraman left but she appreciated his kindness right now. His hand was a warm anchor that was the only thing steadying her at this point.

"So this challenge is all about escaping." Axel tilted his head to the supplies. "There are enough supplies to last you the next six days if you don't figure out how to get out of the basement prison, but I really hope you don't need them."

He'd said it. Prison. Her gaze was drawn back to the bars.

Those awful, cold, terrifying bars. They were going to be locked in this cold, disturbing dungeon. Tanner's grip on her hand tightened and she could feel how tight and uncomfortable he was. It comforted her that even this tough military man wasn't impervious to the darkness and anguish here. The thought of being locked in this chilling space was horrifying.

"First you have to break out of this dungeon. Second you have to break out of the house."

Couldn't they just walk back out the front door?

"All the doors and windows will be barred shut," Axel explained, not unkindly but his natural exuberance and smile were gone. He knew how serious this was. "But you have free reign to break through a wall if you can."

Tanner nodded seriously.

"Last of all you have to escape from the island. As soon as you're out of the bay and safely waiting in open water you call me from this phone." He gestured to a phone on the table. It looked like your average cell phone. As long as it worked she didn't care how fancy it was. "If you have any emergency please call as well. We want this to be a challenge but we don't want you hurt. There are cameras throughout the house and island so you don't have to worry about recording anything. Any questions?"

Rania couldn't even think what the first question would be. She just wanted to get the first part over with and hoped Tanner was good at breaking through iron bars. What if they couldn't escape even this first step. Six days of abject, terrifying misery stretched before them. What if she broke down, grabbed the phone, and forfeited her challenge? That did give her a question she had to ask, "If I fail on the challenge, Tanner still gets his money, correct?"

"Yes." Axel smiled then. "He's been hired to protect and help you in any way but the money has already been deposited into his bank account. I look forwarding to depositing yours in your account."

Rania took a deep breath and prayed inside. She could do this. She had to do this. It wasn't for her but for many children, teenagers, men, and women who were captives throughout the world. Captive like she'd be soon. It would definitely give her some empathy to be shut in here. They'd have food and water, beds, chairs, and a working toilet. Most importantly she'd have Tanner. A few minutes ago she hadn't liked him very much but being cast into prison would definitely change perspectives.

"I look forward to it too," she said, trying to sound feisty and sassy but being locked in here had knocked a lot of that out of her. She always tried to act tough to hide how much it had hurt for everyone to turn their backs on her because of Brian's lies. She'd think after three years that hurt would fade but sometimes it reared up and made her feel insecure and unwanted all over again.

"All right, I hate to leave you two but I'm excited to hear and see your week. There are cameras everywhere but if you pull the curtain around the toilet there is no camera angled that direction."

They both nodded.

Axel warmly shook both of their hands again, giving Tanner a final slap on the shoulder then he walked from the cell. "Man, this is as rough as I thought it would be," he muttered as he slid the metal doors closed. He slid them softly but the bang still seemed to radiate throughout the area. He secured a padlock through the door and the bars. "Good luck you two." He lifted a hand in farewell then his light bobbed and disappeared up the stairs with the cameraman following.

The door at the top of the stairs shut with a resounding click and the sound of a lock turning and then their footsteps treaded above them. One final loud shut of the front door and a banging started as someone secured boards into place.

Rania pulled in a shuddering breath and clung to Tanner's hand. She tried to pull in another breath but she couldn't get the oxygen in fast enough. Darkness edged around her vision and Tanner's face seemed to bob in and out with the light from the table.

"I don't think I can do this," she murmured, and then she felt herself falling.

———

Keep reading here.

ALSO BY CAMI CHECKETTS

Survive the Romance

Romancing the Treasure

Romancing the Escape

Romancing the Boat

Mystical Lake Resort Romance

Only Her Undercover Spy

Only Her Cowboy

Only Her Best Friend

Only Her Blue-Collar Billionaire

Only Her Injured Stuntman

Only Her Amnesiac Fake Fiancé

Only Her Hockey Legend

Only Her Smokejumper Firefighter

Only Her Christmas Miracle

Jewel Family Romance

Do Marry Your Billionaire Boss

Do Trust Your Special Ops Bodyguard

Do Date Your Handsome Rival

Do Rely on Your Protector

Do Kiss the Superstar

Do Tease the Charming Billionaire

Do Claim the Tempting Athlete

A Touch of Love: Summer in Snow Valley

Running from the Cowboy: Spring in Snow Valley

Light in Your Eyes: Winter in Snow Valley

Romancing the Singer: Return to Snow Valley

Fighting for Love: Return to Snow Valley

Other Books by Cami

Seeking Mr. Debonair: Jane Austen Pact

Seeking Mr. Dependable: Jane Austen Pact

Saving Sycamore Bay

Oh, Come On, Be Faithful

Protect This

Blog This

Redeem This

The Broken Path

Dead Running

Dying to Run

Fourth of July

Love & Loss

Love & Lies

ABOUT THE AUTHOR

Cami is a part-time author, part-time exercise consultant, part-time housekeeper, full-time wife, and overtime mother of four adorable boys. Sleep and relaxation are fond memories. She's never been happier.

Join Cami's VIP list to find out about special deals, giveaways and new releases and receive a free copy of *Seeking Mr. Debonair: The Jane Austen Pact* by clicking here.

cami@camichecketts.com
www.camichecketts.com